For all the misfits

THE RED HOT EARL

The Earl of Buckleigh was once an untitled misfit, tormented at Oxford. Now, he's overcome his challenges and is eager for the future, especially when his oldest and dearest friend, Bianca, needs help to save the annual holiday party. Ash has a plan to rescue the event, but when the bullies from his youth are up to their old tricks, he must risk everything to put the past behind him and find true love.

Furious when her brother refuses to host the St. Stephen's Day party, Lady Bianca Stafford is committed to giving the villagers their celebration. In Ash, she sees salvation for their local tradition, and perhaps a future she never expected. But her brother has other plans for her—a Season and marriage, and not to Ash. When disaster strikes, everything she cares about is threatened and it will take a miracle—or a hero—to save the day.

The Red Hot Earl is inspired by the song and story, Rudolph the Red-Nosed Reindeer. Be sure to check out the Red Hot Earl version of the song on my website at darcyburke.com!

Don't miss the rest of Love is All Around, a Regency Holiday Trilogy about the Stafford siblings!

Meet the youngest sister, Bianca Stafford in The Red Hot Earl!

Next up is the middle sibling, Poppy Stafford Kirkwood in The Gift of the Marquess!

Finally, don't miss the exciting conclusion to this holiday saga with their older brother Calder Stafford, the Duke of Hartwell in Joy to the Duke!

Love romance? Have a free book (or two or three) on me!

Sign up at http://www.darcyburke.com/readerclub for members-only exclusives, including advance notice of pre-orders and insider scoop, as well as contests, giveaways, freebies, and 99 cent deals!

Want to share your love of my books with like-minded readers? Want to hang with me and get inside scoop? Then don't miss my exclusive Facebook groups!

Darcy's Duchesses for historical readers
Burke's Book Lovers for contemporary readers

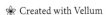

CHAPTER 1

"Come to Thornaby's house party with me. Please." Lady Bianca Stafford didn't want to beg her brother, but she was close to doing so.

Calder Stafford, the eighth Duke of Hartwell, pressed his lips into a thin white line, absolutely unmoved by her passionate pleas. "There is no reason for me to attend, nor do I have any desire."

Bianca walked around his desk, forcing him to turn his head to follow her movements. She stood next to his chair and gave him her most earnest stare. "There's every reason. This is the start of the holiday season. It's where the informal planning for the annual St. Stephen's Day party happens. You *must* come."

He pinched the bridge of his aquiline nose. "Bianca, I am not going to host a St. Stephen's Day party."

She couldn't keep herself from gasping. "You can't be serious. We always host the St. Stephen's

Day party." It wasn't *a* party, it was *the* party. The entire town came, and it was the very center of the Christmas season.

He dropped his hand to the arm of his chair and stared up at her unblinking, his dark gray eyes as cold and unyielding as the nickname some still used for him: Chill. Because he'd been the Earl of Chilton his whole life. Until their father's death seven months ago.

Regret and sadness squeezed Bianca's heart, because of the loss of their father and because of the vast breach between him and Calder that had never been healed.

"*I* am not hosting it, and that is the end of it." His tone was soft but sharp.

She gaped at him, unable to find words for what seemed an eternity. "But, but—" she stuttered before snapping her lips closed at the distaste in her brother's eyes. How he'd become such a remote, unfeeling person was beyond her. But then she'd rarely seen him the past ten years while he'd lived in London. He'd never come home, not once.

Taking a deep breath, she sought to calm her racing heart and outraged mind. "Calder." She used the name their sister Poppy had always called him. The name their mother, who had died a few days after giving birth to Bianca, had used, or so Poppy had told her. "You have a duty as the duke."

"I have many duties, and none of them include hosting a St. Stephen's Day party." He turned his attention back to his desk and the papers upon it. "Now, run along to your house party."

His condescending tone grated. She would go as soon as Poppy, who was the Marchioness of Darlington, arrived to act as her chaperone. "Your tenants adore the St. Stephen's Day party. It is the highlight of their year. Surely that's important."

He didn't look up. "It is not."

Grumbling low in her throat, Bianca glared at her older brother's bent head. "Papa would be disappointed. He's likely spinning in his grave."

Silence was her answer, and so she turned and stalked from his study, not stopping until she nearly ran into Poppy in the entrance hall.

"Goodness, you look as if you want to commit murder," Poppy said, her gray-blue eyes wide. "Well, perhaps not murder. That's rather gruesome."

"In this case, however, it's accurate. I would cheerfully choke our brother if I could manage it."

Poppy exhaled. "Should I go and speak with him?"

"You don't even know why I wish to strangle him," Bianca said.

"I feel certain you will tell me."

"Yes, yes, I talk too much." Bianca waved her hand. "In this case, I could talk until my tongue fell out, and I'm afraid it wouldn't matter. Calder refuses to host the St. Stephen's Day party." Just saying it aloud deepened her anger.

Poppy's delicate dark brows arched high upon her forehead. "You found this surprising given his behavior the past six months since he returned?"

"Yes." But she shouldn't have. Still, she'd hoped. "How can he not care about the tenants and how important that day is to them?" The day after Christmas, it was a time for everyone in and around the village of Hartwell and the estate of Hartwood to come together and celebrate, to cast off their cares and responsibilities and rejoice in fellowship and love.

"The day can still be important. It will just be up to you to make it that way." Poppy gave her a supportive smile. "I would offer to help, but…" Her voice faltered, and a shadow dashed through her eyes.

Bianca reached for her sister's gloved hand and gave it a squeeze. "I wouldn't ask." Poppy was going through a difficult time, and it was more than enough that she'd consented to accompany Bianca to this three-day party at Thornhill, the Viscount Thornaby's estate an hour away.

"Thank you, darling," Poppy said, squeezing her hand in return. "The footman is loading your luggage onto my coach. Are you ready?"

"I am." Bianca cast a sad look back toward their brother's study. She still had time to change his mind. But not much.

Her maid, Donnelly, entered the hall with Bianca's accessories. When she'd donned her hat, cape, and gloves, they departed the house. The Darlington coach awaited them outside, Poppy's maid ensconced within.

Once they were on their way, Bianca turned toward her sister, her mind churning. "We'll have to be careful not to reveal Calder's hesitance to host the party. I don't want anyone to know he was against it, even for a moment."

Poppy blinked at her, then pursed her lips. "Bianca, he *is* against it. And not just for a moment. He isn't going to change his decision. You must let it go, unfortunately."

"I refuse. It's tradition—the village of Hartwell will be devastated if it doesn't go on as it has for the past... I don't know how long."

"I've heard there has been a celebration of some kind since the first duke, even under Cromwell when it was forbidden to celebrate Christmas." Poppy glanced out the window, a dark curl bobbing against her temple beneath the brim of her smart pine-green bonnet. "However, Calder is the duke now. It is up to him to continue the tradition. Or not."

Frustrated at her sister's lack of outrage, Bianca stared at the passing landscape. The fields were hard and barren with the onset of winter, the hedges rich and green beneath the naked branches of the trees. Turning her head to look at her sister once more, she asked, "Aren't you the least bit disappointed?"

"Of course I am. But I am far more disappointed with other matters." She looked out the window and murmured, "Never mind."

Bianca tamped down her irritation. Poppy had other concerns. "I apologize. This isn't your worry. It's mine." And she'd ensure the party happened. She had to. Maybe Calder didn't care about tradition or about spreading goodwill amongst the people of Hartwell and the retainers and tenants of Hartwood, but Bianca did.

Several minutes passed before Poppy made a quiet observation. "I can see your mind working."

Bianca's mouth tilted into a half smile in spite of herself. "Can you?"

Poppy chuckled softly. "It never stops. And that is a compliment. Your ever-turning brain is what makes you Bianca."

It also made her unwed. Most gentlemen, it turned out, did not care for a wife with excessive opinions and a penchant for sharing them. Not that she'd spent much time concerning herself with finding a husband.

At twenty-two, she was a tad overdue on the Marriage Mart, owing to her father's illness the past few years. Beyond that, she had no desire to have a Season in London. She loved Hartwell and the surrounding area, and, if she *had* to marry— and she wasn't certain she did—would much prefer to marry a local gentleman. The problem was that there weren't very many of them who hadn't gone off to war. There would be several at the house party, however, including Viscount Thornaby himself.

She didn't want to marry Thornaby or anyone else at this juncture, but perhaps he would be interested in taking up where Calder refused regarding the party. Thornhill was an hour by carriage, and even longer by foot, which made the location less than ideal, but if it was all she could find… Yes, she'd take the opportunity of this house party to devise a contingency plan. Just in case Calder proved exceptionally stubborn.

Or coldhearted.

She feared it was the latter. The brother who'd returned from London was not the brother she remembered from her youth. But then neither was her sister. She slid a look at Poppy. Faint lines pulled at her eyes and mouth as she gazed out the window, making her look slightly older than her twenty-four years. Bianca wished her sister would share more of her struggles, but she didn't.

Sometimes Bianca wondered if she wasn't really from the same family as her older brother and sister. Both Calder and Poppy held their emotions close, while Bianca displayed hers for everyone to see. Papa had said she was just like her mother. How Bianca wished she could have known that for herself.

Oh, this was turning into a melancholy day! Bianca straightened her shoulders and pressed her spine against the squab. It was nearly her favorite time of year—the time when people were more apt to share themselves and find joy. A time of peace and happiness.

And she wouldn't let Calder ruin it. The St.

Stephen's Day party would happen at Hartwood. She refused to accept anything else.

~

Standing in the drawing room of Thornhill, the Viscount Thornaby's country home, Ashton Rutledge, Earl of Buckleigh, took a deep breath and counted to three. The exercise came easily after so many years, and he prayed it would work as well as it typically did. When he didn't cough or grunt or angle his head, he knew it had, and he thanked heaven for it.

He smiled blandly at his host, Thornaby. "Thank you for the invitation."

"Couldn't ignore the new earl!" Thornaby chuckled, but it wasn't jovial. Perhaps it was the way his gaze darted to his friends, Keldon and Moreley, or the underlying smirk teasing his thin lips.

Ash swallowed the response he wanted to give —*I'm sure you tried*—and worked to focus on the future rather than the past. Perhaps they'd all grown up—as he had.

"Must say you aren't at all what I remembered," Moreley said, sizing Ash up and seeming perplexed by what he saw.

Ash could well imagine what Moreley and the others were thinking, that Ash scarcely resembled the scrawny boy who'd finished Oxford ahead of them ten years ago. "I would say the same of you," Ash responded as he took in Moreley's receding hairline, Keldon's slight paunch, and Thornaby's... what? He looked much the same. Still tall and angular, his nose long, and his eyes small and hungry.

"Could you?" Keldon said, glancing at his friends. "We haven't changed at all." The others nodded and laughed amongst themselves as if they were sharing a jest that only the three of them were privy to.

Well, that was discouraging. Change, Ash had long ago decided, was an excellent thing.

Moreley sniffed. "Won't lie to you. We miss Lyndon terribly."

Ash kept from scowling, both to keep from insulting the trio before him and because it wasn't polite to think ill of the dead. But it was blessed hard not to think ill of the former earl, his morally bankrupt cousin. Ash heard his mother's voice, a constant refrain in his youth: *"We must pity poor Lyndon for he didn't have the love and support you did. To be raised without a mother and with a cold, dispassionate father is a tragedy in and of itself."*

It hadn't made Lyndon's abuse of Ash any easier to suffer.

But that was the past, and Ash meant to concentrate on the future. No matter how difficult, especially here and now, when the past was in his face.

"I'm sure Lyndon would rather he was here with you," Ash said evenly.

Thornaby snorted. "That's bloody obvious."

"We will shoot tomorrow in his honor," Moreley said, his voice lifting in tribute. He cast a pitying look toward Ash. "Too bad you can't join in."

That had been true once, and Ash supposed it still was, in a way. "I can, however I choose not to." He was new to the earldom, and hunting for sport was not something he'd ever done, nor was it something he particularly desired to learn. He could, contrary to their assumption, ride *and* shoot.

Moreley's dark gaze flickered with surprise, and he exchanged knowing glances with his friends before returning his attention to Ash. "You can remain here with the ladies. Perhaps they will allow you to play piquet."

Keldon snickered. "The perfect solution."

"Or you could arrange for me, and anyone else who prefers not to hunt, to ride," Ash suggested smoothly, looking toward his host.

Unfortunately, the butler interrupted the conversation before Thornaby could respond.

"Lady Darlington and Lady Bianca Stafford, my lord," the butler said before stepping aside as the two women he'd announced moved into the drawing room.

Though it had been years since he'd seen both ladies, Ash recognized them immediately. Lady Darlington was slightly taller with gray-blue eyes that assessed her surroundings and a reserved demeanor evidenced in her stiff, compact stance with her hands clasped together at her waist.

Lady Bianca, on the other hand, seemed to brim with enthusiasm. She took a step toward them, her bright blue eyes sparkling with curiosity and verve. Though small, she seemed a mass of tightly controlled energy, her legs slightly parted, her hands at her sides as if she might sprint forward at any moment. Dark curls framed her heart-shaped face.

Thornaby bowed. "Welcome to Thornhill, Lady Darlington, Lady Bianca."

The other gentlemen bowed and murmured a welcome. Ash stepped toward the marchioness and offered his leg. "It's a pleasure to see you again, Lady Darlington." Then he turned and gave the same bow to her younger sister. "Lady Bianca."

"I'm afraid I don't—" Whatever Lady Darlington had been about to say was cut off by Keldon.

"This is the new Earl of Buckleigh," Keldon

said. "He was Lyndon's cousin. Surely you remember the red hair."

Lady Darlington smiled as she shook her head in bemusement. "How silly of me. It's lovely to see you again, my lord."

"Ash?" Lady Bianca said, stepping toward him. "I didn't recognize you at all! We were so sorry to hear about Lyndon's passing. I'd heard you'd inherited and were now at Buck Manor."

She remembered him. And she called him Ash without reserve or remorse. It was right that she called him that, for in their youth, he'd been Ash and she'd been Bee.

"Yes, I'm there now. It feels a bit…odd." Perhaps he shouldn't have admitted that out loud, but this was Bee, the girl who'd followed him around one summer collecting insects and climbing trees.

"Odd?" Thornaby said with more volume than was necessary. "I should think it would be lovely. An improvement, to be sure."

"Perhaps not," Bee said with a shrug. "Ash is entitled to feel as he ought." She gave him a warm smile that lit her eyes. "I imagine it would be odd— Buck Manor, the earldom, all of it. You cut a fine figure of an earl," she added, her gaze surveying him with approval.

Bloody hell, but she was direct and absolutely without guile. Ash hadn't been sure such people existed.

Then she turned abruptly to their host and subjected Thornaby to the same perusal. "We'd like to take a rest before dinner. What time shall we come down?" It was as if she were in charge. Ash suppressed a smile.

"Six," Thornaby said, glancing between Bee and her sister.

"Excellent. And may we expect dancing after?"

"For those who are able." Thornaby cast a disdainful stare toward Ash, whose shoulders twitched in response.

Ash gritted his teeth, and every muscle in his body tensed.

Bee's vivid blue eyes narrowed as she slanted a glance at Ash and then fixed on their host. "I can't imagine what you mean by that, but I shall presume there will be entertainment to amuse everyone. If not, I'll see that there is."

Thornaby bowed slightly. "I would be honored, Lady Bianca. I am without a hostess, and if you would like to claim that role—"

"You overstep," Lady Darlington said crisply. "Come, Bianca." She gave Thornaby a scolding glare before taking her sister's arm and retreating from the room.

"She's a lively one!" Keldon said on a laugh.

Thornaby smoothed the front of his coat. "I know for a fact that Hartwell wants to be rid of her as soon as possible, preferably before he has to provide her with a Season. This party is an excellent opportunity."

Moreley flashed a smile displaying his horrendously crooked teeth. "Indeed, the timing is perfect. Do let us know how we can assist you in your pursuit."

Ahem, you are aware that I am standing right here? Ash didn't ask the question aloud, but it was a near thing. Instead, he took another deep breath, counted to three, and said, "You'll need a very solid plan to win the Lady Bianca. She told me once, years ago when I lived near Hartwell, that she would never wed." *Never, ever, ever* had been her precise pronouncement, followed by her making a nasty face that looked as if she'd eaten a slug.

Had that been the day she'd licked a slug? He couldn't quite recall.

Keldon peered at Ash as if he were a…slug. "You can't mean to reference something she said as a child. In any case, her guardian, and in this case, it's her brother, will dictate what she does."

"That's the right of it," Thornaby said smugly. "And based on that, I would say this courtship will proceed exactly as I expect."

Unable to stand another moment of their arrogance and self-absorption, Ash excused himself and went to the entry, where other guests were arriving. He waited patiently for the butler, who asked if he was ready to be shown to his room.

"Yes, please." As he ascended the stairs, he questioned why he'd come.

Because you're the earl, and earls attend house parties.

Ugh.

Because they are your neighbors—sort of—and you ought to get to know them.

Gah.

Because you have something to prove.

He tightened his hands into fists, a familiar reaction given how he'd spent the last ten years of his life in London. No, he had nothing to prove, especially to those "gentlemen" he'd left downstairs.

The butler led him into a large sitting room with several doors leading from it. "Here you are, my lord," the butler said, opening one of the doors. "Will there be anything else?"

Ash glanced inside and caught a glimpse of Harris, his valet. "No, thank you."

With a nod, the butler left, and Ash went into the bedchamber, closing the door behind him.

"All unpacked, my lord," Harris said with his usual ebullient efficiency. Just twenty-one, he was likely a poor choice for a valet, but Lyndon's had left after he'd died, necessitating the hiring of a new one. Since Ash had little experience with hiring valets, he'd simply promoted the most pleasant, eager footman he could find.

Attitude could not be taught. Everything else could.

"Thank you, Harris. We have some time until dinner. I suppose I shall read." And devise a plan to rescue Bee from Thornaby's pursuit. If she wanted to be rescued. Perhaps she'd changed her mind about marriage. Thornaby was right that she couldn't be held to something she'd said as a child.

Yet, the woman he'd seen downstairs seemed every bit the confident, outrageous young girl he remembered. The type of woman who listened to the rules and then promptly bent them to suit herself. The type of woman who could stir something deep inside him if he allowed himself to respond.

Ash began to remove his coat, and Harris darted toward him to help. Once Harris draped the coat over his arm, Ash tugged at his cravat and handed it to the valet as well. "That will suffice," Ash said, and Harris took himself into the small dressing chamber.

Turning toward the hearth, Ash noted that Harris had placed his book of poetry on a table beside a chair. Ash sat and plucked up the book, opening it, but then didn't read. Instead, he thought of Bee and how wonderful it was to see her again.

If I allow myself to respond…

He would *not*.

CHAPTER 2

*D*inner dragged a course too long, but then Bianca often felt that was the case. She never wanted to eat as much as was offered or sit as long as was expected. By the time the ladies removed to the drawing room, she was more than ready for the entertainment to begin.

More importantly, she was eager to discuss St. Stephen's Day with Viscount Thornaby. She'd sat beside him at dinner, but every time she'd tried to broach the topic of the St. Stephen's Day party, he'd waved it off and said they'd discuss it later, then asked her some inane question. Did she paint? Did she like to ride? Did she enjoy the theatre? Was she looking forward to going to London?

No. Yes. She couldn't say—because she'd only been to the theatre once. And definitely *not*.

Poppy walked with her into the drawing room and went toward a settee.

"I can't sit just yet," Bianca said.

"Of course not. I forget you are typically wound full of energy after a long meal." She shook her head, smiling. "How I could forget that is a mystery."

Bianca touched her arm gently. "You have a great deal on your mind."

Poppy didn't respond, but her expression was grateful.

Mrs. Chamberlain and her daughter, who was a couple of years younger than Bianca, approached them. "We're sorry the duke didn't come with you," Mrs. Chamberlain said. "He must be terribly busy now that he's inherited."

She had the terrible part right. "Yes," Bianca responded. What else could she say? That he'd wanted to come but couldn't get away? She supposed that would suffice, but he didn't deserve excuses. Let people think what they wanted.

"Well, I imagine we'll see him at the assembly next month and on St. Stephen's Day after that." Mrs. Chamberlain looked proudly at her daughter. "I wonder if he'll remember my Marianne."

Bianca opened her mouth to tell the poor woman to forget about any hope of snagging Calder, but Poppy spoke first. "I imagine he will. If you'll excuse us?" She offered a benign smile, then roped her arm through Bianca's and ushered her away.

"You can't think Calder will actually attend the assembly, not with the way he's been acting."

"I don't, but neither is it our place to say so." Poppy frowned. "However, perhaps we should mention that the St. Stephen's Day party will not be happening."

"No!" Bianca kept her voice low but urgent. "I said we mustn't let anyone know."

Poppy took her hand. "And I told you that you aren't going to change his mind. The sooner you accept that the party isn't happening this year, the better off you will be. In fact, if Calder's manner doesn't improve, and honestly, I can't see it doing so, you should come spend Christmas with us."

Oh, that was precisely what Bianca wanted to do—insert herself into her and Gabriel's household when Poppy was suffocating in despair. "Thank you, but Hartwell is my home, and as such, I should have a say in what is done there, including whether there is a St. Stephen's Day party or not."

Staring at Bianca in disbelief, Poppy said, "You can't host it without Calder's permission. How would you even pay for it? And that's just the beginning. The staff won't go against him."

"But they will want to have the party!" Bianca's frustration grew even as she knew Poppy was right. She couldn't hold the party without Calder's support.

Bianca wasn't sure she was still in the mood for entertainment. Naturally, this was when the gentlemen entered the drawing room. Her gaze instantly found Ash, perhaps because of his magnificent red hair. She'd always found it fascinating. Her hair and that of her siblings was dark and still and boring. But Ash's was light and fire and energy.

"Lord Buckleigh appears quite different," Poppy murmured.

"Does he?" Bianca asked, her gaze still lingering on him.

"Don't you remember what he was like? He had trouble with words and he would…twitch."

Bianca tried to recall but couldn't. She shook her head. "That doesn't sound like the Ash I knew."

"It was later, just before he was sent off to school with his cousin," Poppy said. "Perhaps I was more aware because I am closer to his age. He was also rather small. Looking at him now, you would never know."

Had he been? Bianca didn't remember that either, but then *she'd* been small, so her perspective was likely different. Whether he'd been small or not, he certainly wasn't now. He was taller than every other man in the room, with broad shoulders and long, athletic legs.

He also didn't have freckles anymore, just bare sculpted cheekbones and a slightly square jaw. His gaze swept the room until it settled on her, and the hint of a smile tugged at the side of his mouth.

Thornaby moved to the pianoforte in the corner. "My sister will play for those who wish to dance." He gestured to an open area near the instrument, from which all the furniture had been cleared. Then he walked directly to Bianca. "May I have the pleasure of the first dance?"

She couldn't say no, and her mood *could* use improvement. "Yes, thank you." She gave him her hand, and they moved to the makeshift dance floor, where they formed a square with another couple.

As the music started, he said, "About the St. Stephen's Day party, how strange it will be not to have it this year."

Bianca fumbled her steps. "What?"

"The St. Stephen's party," Thornaby repeated, looking at her in slight confusion. "The duke sent me a letter indicating it would not be happening. I presumed that's what you kept trying to talk about at dinner."

So he had been changing the subject on purpose despite the fact that she'd clearly wanted to discuss it. She gritted her teeth. Her mood was *not* improved. There was also no hope for keeping Calder's decision quiet until she could change his mind. "I'm surprised he wrote to you. We've still been discussing whether to hold it."

"Ah, well, I will need to know soon because we

make arrangements well in advance." His family provided food and ale for the celebration, as did a handful of other local families from the gentry.

"Did you say the St. Stephen's Day party isn't happening?" the other young woman in their square asked. She was Miss Keldon, and her partner was Mr. Lamphrey.

"That is correct," Thornaby said.

"It isn't quite," Bianca contradicted. "My brother is mulling whether to host it. He's a trifle overwhelmed by the dukedom, and I just need to convince him we can handle the event." She offered what she hoped was a serene smile, though her insides were a tumbling riot. Calder would not be pleased if he heard she'd said he was overwhelmed. He would say that once again her mouth had run faster than her brain.

She met Thornaby in the center of the square, and he touched his hands to hers before they retreated. "He sounded rather firm in his letter," Thornaby said. "It's not the end of the world. It's a massive event to undertake. My father always said he was glad he wasn't the Duke of Hartwell so he didn't have to do it!" He laughed, and Lamphrey joined in.

"Well, my father enjoyed it," Bianca said tersely. "As did I. And our retainers and tenants. And the entire town."

"I liked it too," Miss Keldon said in solidarity.

"Alas, all good things must come to an end." Thornaby's tone held a superior note. He looked toward Lamphrey. "Who said that?"

"Shakespeare," Lamphrey said with confidence.

"Actually, it originated with Chaucer," Bianca said with some disgust. She suffered the rest of the dance and quickly made her way back to her sister. Who was talking with Ash.

He smiled warmly as Bianca approached, and some of her agitation washed away. Not all of it, though. She looked to Poppy. "Calder sent a note to everyone about not hosting the party."

Poppy exhaled softly and gave her a look of sympathy. "I suppose that's that, then."

"You can't think I'll stop trying?"

With a light chuckle, Poppy lifted her hands. "I should know better."

"What party?" Ash asked, appearing confused.

"The annual St. Stephen's Day party," Poppy answered.

Ash nodded. "I remember that. Huge affair out at Hartwood. Food, games, revelry regardless of the weather. I missed it when I moved to London. I take it this is the first year it's not happening?"

"Like you, our brother inherited his title this year, and he's decided not to host it." Bianca furrowed her brow. "I am trying to change his mind. Everyone looks forward to it, and it's not as if we can't afford it."

Poppy's brows arched as she cast a look at Bianca that seemed to ask, *Are you certain of that?*

Of course she was certain. Before their father had died, he'd told Bianca of her large settlement, which would be her dowry. Unless she didn't wed. Then it would become hers on her twenty-fifth birthday. She doubted she would have such a substantial sum if the dukedom was not in excellent financial order.

"If anyone can change his mind, I'm certain it's you," Ash said encouragingly. He glanced toward the dance floor. "We've missed this dance, but may I request the honor of partnering you in the next one?"

Again, she couldn't really say no without appearing rude, but she didn't want to be trapped in a square with Thornaby or stand next to him in line. "Actually, would you mind taking a promenade instead? I don't think I have the stomach for another dance."

His gaze flickered with surprise and seemed to hesitate before he answered. "Certainly." He offered her his arm and looked toward Poppy who inclined her head.

Bianca placed her hand on his arm, and they started to circuit the drawing room. "This won't be a very long promenade. We'll have to make two circuits."

"At least."

She responded to the humor in his voice with a grin. "How lovely it is to have you back. Did you ever imagine you would be the earl?"

He shook his head. "I suppose I should have after my uncle died a couple of years ago, but I assumed Lyndon would wed and have sons, and that would be that."

"He called on me early last spring." Bianca recalled Lyndon's attempts to charm her, but she'd been too wrapped up in caring for her father to pay close attention. In fact, she'd asked him not to call again. "I think he hoped to make a match."

"And failed miserably, apparently."

"It wasn't his fault. My father was ill. It wasn't a good time." Oh dear, that sounded as if Lyndon's suit might have been appreciated, and she was fairly certain she would have put him off regardless of what was going on in her life.

He shot her a look of apology. "My condolences. I always liked your father."

"Thank you. Goodness, he and your cousin died within a month of each other."

"Did they?" Ash cocked his head to the side. "I think you're right. It's good you didn't wed my cousin—a double tragedy would have been horrible."

"There was no danger of that, even if my father had been well. I don't think your cousin and I would have suited. Actually, I'm not sure marriage is for me."

He laughed, surprising her. "You swore never to marry."

She laughed too. "You remember that?"

His gaze met hers. "I remember many things."

An unfamiliar heat bloomed in her chest and spread. She turned her head from his. "That's one circuit."

"It is indeed. I should warn you that Thornaby has his sights set on courting you. He means to make himself known at this party, if I'm not mistaken."

She didn't stop herself before pulling a face. "I hope you're wrong."

"I don't think I am."

She thought of her dance with Thornaby and sighed with disgust. "No, I don't think you are either." She cast him a sidelong glance. "What did he say?"

"You want me to speak freely?"

She lifted a shoulder. "We always did."

"We were children."

"Such a shame that children can say whatever they like to each other, and when we become adults, we must hesitate and consider and censor." She gave him a sly look. "I'm not very good at that, I'm afraid."

He chuckled. "I wouldn't expect you to be—not the Bee I remember."

"Are you going to tell me what Thornaby said or not?"

He grinned. "He said your brother is anxious to

marry you off, preferably before he has to pay for a Season. I can't believe that's true—it's just Thornaby being a jackanapes." He flicked her a glance, his eyes widening slightly. "My apologies," he murmured.

"No apology is necessary. Thornaby *is* a jackanapes, as far as I can tell. And sadly, that sounds exactly like my brother. He's actually rather horrid." She waved her hand. "Not that it signifies since I don't want a Season anyway. London doesn't interest me." She peered at him. "You lived there?"

"For ten years."

"And you liked it?"

"Very much."

"Why?" She genuinely wanted to know.

"That is a rather lengthy tale, and we are nearly at the end of our second circuit."

Bianca thrust her lips into a mock pout. "That is hardly fair. Will you tell me some other time?"

"It would be my pleasure."

They arrived at Poppy, and Bianca reluctantly pulled her hand from him and moved to stand beside her sister. What a refreshingly honest and open conversation. "Are you going on the hunt in the morning?" Bianca asked.

He shook his head. "I don't hunt."

Bianca's heart thumped an extra beat. She'd never understood hunting for sport with the hounds and all that nonsense. "Oh?"

"I do like to shoot, however, and ride, and I tried to convince Thornaby to organize an excursion for those of us who aren't hunting. I don't think he listened, however."

"Then allow me," Bianca said, narrowing her eyes. "I will see you tomorrow." She turned abruptly and made her way to Thornaby, who'd just left the dance floor.

In five minutes, he'd agreed to organize a ride during the hunt and a separate shooting competition in the afternoon. As she walked back to Poppy, she realized she could likely manipulate him into hosting the St. Stephen's Day party. If she wanted to.

She wasn't sure she did. He would be a ghastly host. Unfortunately, she might not have any other choice.

Her gaze trailed to where Ash stood talking to a pair of young ladies. He would be a *much* better host. Except his estate was too far away. They'd have to transport everyone over ten miles.

Bianca's brain began to churn...

"You're thinking again," Poppy said, eyeing her speculatively.

A grin slid over Bianca's lips. "Always."

~

*T*he morning was slightly overcast and quite cold. As a result, only two people showed up for the ride—Ash and Bee. There were more grooms to accompany them, three to be exact.

Ash wondered if she'd beg off since it would be just them. Instead, she seemed...pleased?

Bee's eyes sparkled in the midmorning light as she glanced around. "Just us, then?"

"So it appears," Ash said.

She gave him an impish smile. "Lovely." She crossed to the mounting block and climbed atop the horse Thornaby had provided.

Ash mounted his horse and moved closer to Bee. "Is this acceptable? Us alone on a ride, I mean."

She shrugged. "Does it matter?"

He laughed. "You are as audacious as I remember."

"Is that a good thing?" she asked as they started out of the stable yard.

"I think so. It's certainly not boring."

"Is that a danger? Boring females?"

"Anything boring is a danger."

"I wholeheartedly agree. What did you do in London to ward off boredom?" she asked. "You promised to tell me why you liked living there."

He sent her a teasing look. "I don't recall promising you anything."

She rolled her eyes. "Perhaps I exaggerate."

"You? Never." He recalled the time she'd said she'd seen a wolf, but when he'd told her there were no wolves in England, she'd admitted it was just a large dog. "I feel the need to run, then I will tell you about London, all right?"

She nodded, then gave him a coy smile. "Shall we race?"

They were out of the stable yard and cresting the small hill that overlooked the parkland adjoining Thornaby's estate. She didn't wait for his response before kicking her horse into a gallop.

"Bloody hell," he muttered in both appreciation and anticipation. He directed his mount after her and did his best to keep up.

She won in the end, but then he hadn't tried too hard to overtake her. He'd enjoyed watching her far too much.

When he caught up to her, she was grinning, her breath coming hard as she stroked her horse's neck. "Caught me at last?"

"You're an exceptional rider," he said.

"Thank you. I didn't get to see you, but since you kept up, I imagine you are also quite skilled."

He laughed at her hubris. "I'm passable."

"Don't denigrate yourself. You're more than that." She started to walk her horse back the way they came, the grooms trailing behind them. "Now tell me about London."

"You've truly never been?"

She shook her head. "My father never encouraged me to go when I was younger, and it didn't occur to me to ask. I'm quite content here in County Durham. But I imagine there is much to do and see in London."

"Oh yes. The theatre. The British Museum. The Royal Academy Exhibition. Hyde Park. And so much more." He thought of his favorite places—nowhere she could go.

"That's what you liked about living there—the places to visit? To alleviate your boredom?" She asked the last with a flirtatious smile.

Flirtatious? Maybe. He wasn't particularly good at flirting and wasn't entirely sure he'd know what it even looked like. He had no experience on the Marriage Mart or in courtship in general. "It was hard to be bored. I was accepted to the Inns of Court and worked as a barrister."

She seemed impressed, her gaze moving over him with admiration. "Well done. What did you do for fun?"

Hit people.

Thankfully, he didn't say that out loud. Boxing had been his true love—a way to work through the anger he'd nurtured for so many years at school and to control his impulses. The speech, the coughing and throat clearing, the twitches.

Not long after he'd arrived in London, he'd attended a match. That had led to lessons and ultimately to participating in matches himself. Nothing glamorous, but small bouts that allowed him to hone his skill and learn self-control. And build a reputation as a fearsome pugilist, which hadn't been his intent.

"I, ah, didn't have much spare time. But I enjoyed riding."

She narrowed her eyes at him. "This is not a long story at all. You were bamming me last night."

"Hmm, you may be right. It was ten years, so it felt like a long story." He tried to think of what he could say that wouldn't reveal too much. She was a young lady, after all.

Hell, she was also *Bee*.

"I loved London," he said, reflecting on how much he'd changed in his time there. "It's where I became who I am. I don't think that would have happened if I'd come back here when I finished at Oxford." He hadn't wanted to anyway, not after everything he'd endured there.

"Becoming a lawyer did that?" she asked, sounding skeptical. "I think there's more to your story. Maybe someday you'll tell me."

He wanted to. "Maybe someday I will."

They trotted their horses for a few minutes, then slowed once more as they approached Thornhill.

"I wonder if you might give me your opinion on something," she said, looking at him askance.

"If I can, I will."

"I wager you know Thornaby better than I. Do you think he'd host the St. Stephen's Day party?"

"Why would—" He caught himself before he finished. Though he worked hard to keep a rein on himself, sometimes things leapt from his mouth. He stretched his neck in reaction. "I don't think I know him well enough to say."

"I hope I didn't anger you with my question."

Hell, he hadn't meant to give her that impression. "Not at all." He sought to divert. "Why isn't your brother hosting the party?"

"I wish I knew. I mean, *really* knew. He just says he won't do it. He doesn't have a good reason. He doesn't have *any* reason, as far as I can tell."

Ash didn't know Calder Stafford very well—he'd been gone from Oxford by the time Ash and Lyndon had arrived, and Ash had only run into him periodically in London. "I'm sorry he's proving difficult. It's such a shame he won't host it. Or at least give you a good reason."

"Yes, he owes us that, if nothing else."

He blinked at her. "Us?"

"Me. Our retainers and tenants. The villagers. You."

"*Me?*"

"You would have come, wouldn't you?"

"Probably." He hadn't thought about the event at all. It was enough to consider spending his first Christmas season as an earl at Buck Manor.

"Is your mother at Buck Manor now? It seems I haven't seen her in Hartwell the last several months."

"She came to join me this past July. She will be disappointed about the party, now that I think about it."

"We must have it," Bee said as they rode back into the stable yard. "Everyone will be disappointed. Calder will have to come around."

"And if he doesn't?"

A groom met them, and Ash dismounted. He quickly handed the reins to the groom, then went to help Bee down.

She'd been on her way to the mounting block but stopped when she saw him approach. The groom took her reins, and she turned to place her hands on Ash's shoulders, then slid from the saddle.

Ash clasped her waist firmly. When she stood before him, he could see the cobalt depths of her eyes and smell the sweet fragrance of her floral soap. A surprising heat stole over him, suffusing him in something he hadn't expected: desire.

Taking his hands from her, he stepped back.

She smoothed her hands down her skirt, seemingly unaffected by their brief connection. And why should she have felt what he had? In fact, he was beginning to doubt he'd felt anything at all. He was simply happy to see her after so many years.

"To answer your question," she said, "if Calder doesn't come around, I must come up with an alternate plan. Though it pains me, I think I must ask Thornaby if he will host it."

Thornaby would be delighted to help her. Except he was also incredibly cheap, or at least he had been, and Ash couldn't imagine that had changed. He was, however, eager to establish a relationship with Bee, and Ash wouldn't put it past the man to try to use her request to benefit himself. "Be careful," he advised.

"I always am." She turned toward the house, a breeze stirring the dark curls about her face.

Ash laughed. "Like when you climbed so high in the tree that I had to come up and help you down?"

"Yes, exactly like that."

He laughed harder. "How is that being careful?"

She flashed him a smile. "Because I knew you were there to rescue me."

The laughter stuck in his throat, but he forced it out lest she realize how her words affected him. And how was that?

"Would the woman you are now actually want to be rescued?"

She stopped and pivoted toward him. "No." She stared up at him. "How could you know that?"

He hadn't, but he'd guessed. She'd always been confident, almost reckless, even. And she seemed as outspoken and fearless as ever. "It made sense that you grew into a someone who can take care of herself."

She looked at him with unflinching pride. "Thank you."

They continued toward the house. "Still, if there is ever any way I can be of assistance, I hope you'll ask."

They reached the doorway and she paused. "I will. Unlike you, I will make a promise. And I will keep it." Her gaze turned saucy, and he had to think she was flirting. Again. Maybe.

"I didn't make you a promise," he repeated softly. "But when I do, I will keep it." He opened the door for her.

She held his gaze a long moment, then the edge of her mouth ticked up. "Good."

CHAPTER 3

*B*ianca and Poppy walked from the house toward the lawn where the shooting competition was set up. Bianca hoped they planned to allow women to participate. And if they didn't, well, she'd shoot anyway.

Most of the house party guests were in attendance. Bianca immediately spotted Ash standing on the periphery of a group of gentlemen.

"It looks like the spectators are over there," Poppy said, gesturing to the right where most of the guests were gathered. Everyone else, including a handful of footmen, was clustered near a table. Beyond that stood three targets. "Do you mean to shoot?" Poppy asked.

"I do."

"Papa would be proud." Poppy's voice was soft. She missed their father, but not as much as Bianca, likely owing to the fact that it was Bianca who had cared for him in his final years. Poppy had already been wed to the Marquess of Darlington. And, of course, Calder had been off in London hardening his heart.

"You could shoot too," Bianca suggested, even though she knew her sister would decline.

Poppy laughed with genuine mirth. "No one wants to see that. I never possessed the skill that you do. Frankly, I never possessed the desire to learn."

"No, you are a much more proper female."

"Because I like to sing and play music?" Poppy gave her a teasing look.

"Because you are good at both and at needlepoint and all things domestic. All the things at which I am abysmal." Bianca grinned with pride.

"That is not true. You are more than capable of arranging and managing all manner of things. That is an exceptional domestic talent."

"I suppose it is." Bianca fixed her gaze on the target field with great intent. "They better allow me to shoot. I don't see one woman over there."

"I fear for them if they don't," Poppy said drily.

Bianca sent her a wicked glance, then strode toward the target area. Ash noted her approach, a single auburn brow arching along his forehead.

"Good afternoon, Lady Bianca," Thornaby said in greeting, his thin lips stretching back to reveal a patronizing smile. No, that wasn't fair. Bianca oughtn't assume they weren't going to let her participate. "Did you come to wish us good luck?" He gazed at her expectantly.

She rocked forward on her toes. "Not at all. I came to shoot."

Thornaby's eyes widened, and someone laughed. Followed by a second person. Then a third. While the viscount didn't join in, he was clearly trying not to smirk. "I'm afraid this competition is for gentlemen only," he said with mild condescension. "You may watch from over there." He motioned toward the spectators.

Bianca forced a sickly sweet smile. "Are you afraid I'll beat you?"

Her query was met with more laughter.

"It's a danger," Mr. Moreley said from the side of his mouth. "She did beat Ruddy in a race earlier. Sorry, Buckleigh, I mean."

Several gentlemen turned their heads toward Ash and snickered. Moreley had said sorry, but he didn't appear apologetic. And Bianca didn't think he'd been apologizing for mentioning the race. No, he'd corrected himself after calling Ash "Ruddy." Was that a nickname?

"Trounced him, I heard," another gentleman said.

Bianca noted that no one looked at her with admiration or appreciation. They all cast taunting glances toward Ash. He stood silent, his face impassive.

"It wasn't a race," Bianca said, even though she'd absolutely challenged him to a race. She'd sensed he hadn't actually raced her.

How had any of them heard about it anyway? She scowled toward the stables, thinking it had to have been one of the grooms. She detested a retainer with loose lips and was glad to have none of those at Hartwell.

"It was, and you won," Ash said, causing everyone to whip their heads in his direction. "I've no problem losing to a woman." He pinned Thornaby with an expectant stare. "Why not let her shoot?"

"Because the prizes aren't for women," he said crossly. He turned back to Bianca and summoned a pathetic excuse for a smile. "Why don't you demonstrate your skill for us prior to the competition?"

"An excellent notion," Ash said. "Her efforts can still be measured against everyone else's." He looked her in the eye, and Bianca had never felt more included or…present. The moment enveloped her until she forced herself to speak.

She turned to Thornaby. "I accept."

Thornaby looked utterly nonplussed. He exchanged a look with one of the other gentlemen, his brow creasing. Bianca held her breath. Would he allow her to shoot, or would he make an even bigger scene?

He settled his gaze on her. "Which weapon would you like to use?" His voice was tight, as if just asking the question pained him.

She had to bite her tongue lest she laugh. And he hoped to court her? Moving past him to the table, she perused the half-dozen weapons laid out. There was a lady's muff pistol in addition to a Manton flintlock. Her father had given her a lady's muff pistol three years ago. It looked small compared to the others, but she knew it was just as powerful. Still, she was surprised to see it on the table with the other weapons since it wasn't generally used for distance shooting. Why would they include it?

Swallowing her smile, she reached for the muff pistol, then frowned. "It's already loaded."

"Of course," the viscount said.

"I prefer to load my own." She didn't press the issue. It was enough that she was allowed to shoot. *Allowed.* Bitterness rose in her throat, and she swallowed it back as she stepped around the table. "Does it matter which target I use?" she asked.

"No, you just have to say which before you shoot," someone other than Thornaby answered.

"The middle one." She lifted the pistol and fixed her aim. Eyeing the target—a piece of crockery atop a post—she squeezed the trigger.

The crockery splintered and flew from the post to a chorus of cheers—from the spectators. And from one of the gentlemen. She turned. It was Ash, of course. He grinned and applauded.

A rush of pleasure swept over Bianca. She dipped a curtsey.

"Lucky shot," Keldon said, staring at the pottery she'd ruined that now littered the ground around the post. He sounded shocked, as if he couldn't believe what he'd seen.

Irritation pricked her neck. "It wasn't luck. Shall I demonstrate again?" she asked with mock innocence. "Perhaps the Manton?"

Thornaby came toward her. "I think that's enough for today. Thank you for the…demonstration."

Bianca bit back a retort. This was why marriage held no interest for her. She'd yet to meet a man who truly valued a woman as a person of equal merit and ability. Her gaze flicked to Ash, who was frowning at Thornaby.

Feeling slightly mollified by Ash's attitude and seeming support, she retreated toward the spectators, though she didn't go all the way. It was a small rebellion at least.

Thornaby looked at where she stood and frowned, but he didn't tell her to move. Good, because she wasn't going to.

One of the footmen reloaded the lady's muff pistol as Thornaby addressed the gentlemen. "We'll have a first round, and everyone who hits the target will proceed to the second round in which we will all fire at the same target. Our shots will be marked, and the one who is closest to the center will be declared the winner."

There were six gentlemen and six pistols. Everyone moved toward the table and plucked up a weapon. Ash was the last to get there and was left with the lady's muff. She so wanted him to best them, but she had no idea if he was a good shot.

Thornaby inclined his head. "I put the lady's pistol out for you. Thought it would be easier for you to manage. Didn't realize an actual woman would want to shoot." He pursed his lips with disdain, and though he'd lowered his voice for the second part, Bianca had still heard him. She was glad she'd stayed relatively near.

"We're willing to let you stand closer, Ruddy," Moreley said toward Ash before looking at the other gentlemen and laughing.

There was that name again. Ruddy had to be Ash, but why? His last name was Rutledge. Was it a nickname? She looked at his temple where his dark red hair peeked from beneath his hat. Ruddy—red.

Ash checked his pistol. "That won't be necessary, but I appreciate your thoughtfulness."

The gentlemen took turns, and it happened that Ash went last. Bianca held her breath as he took his stance toward the target.

"The one on the left," Ash responded.

Bianca had to listen carefully to hear all that they said. She was glad she hadn't gone to stand with the others, for she wouldn't be able to hear them at all.

"That's all that remains," Keldon said with amusement.

Ash turned a stony stare toward Keldon. "I am following the rules as directed."

Moreley chuckled. "You always did, even when it wasn't to your benefit."

Ash's jacket rippled across his shoulders, and his head tipped briefly to the side. Then he coughed.

"Oh dear," Keldon said. "Moreley, you've disturbed him. You know better than to do that."

Before anyone could say anything else, Ash fired, and the small pot shattered.

Bianca exhaled and smiled in relief. "Well done!"

Ash turned to look at her, but his features were inscrutable. He seemed very focused, which was good. She wanted him to win.

"Looks like all six of us are progressing," Thornaby pronounced.

Three of the footmen finished reloading the weapons while the other two went to nail a target —a large piece of wood with a small mark in the center—to the posts. They returned to the table, and all was ready for the final round.

How Bianca wished she could participate. It bloody wasn't fair.

"It's a shame Lady Bianca can't be included," Ash said.

One of the gentlemen, a portly fellow called Tealman, glanced toward her, then lowered his voice to say, "It wouldn't be borne." Bianca had to strain to hear. She didn't bother glaring at him despite the anger bubbling in her veins.

Ash chuckled. "As I said, I'm not bothered by the prospect of losing to a woman."

"Clearly, as evidenced by your pathetic loss this morning," Moreley said with considerable disdain.

Bianca wanted to put Moreley in front of the target.

The first man took his place and fired. He struck several inches from the mark and dipped his head slightly as he turned back toward the others. Even so, they congratulated him.

"You've a steady arm," Keldon said, clapping

him on the shoulder. "Better than some." He inclined his head toward Ash.

How dare he say that? Ash had hit the target! And he'd been steady. Bianca's hands balled into fists at her side as she seethed with outrage.

Moreley walked around the table to take his turn. "I have to say, Ruddy's better than he was ten years ago. I daresay he wouldn't have been able to lift the pistol without suffering a fit." He looked back at Ash. "What sorcery have you invited to be so changed?"

"Is he that changed, truly?" Keldon asked. "The speech is better, but I see he still twitches."

"Perhaps he drinks," Thornaby offered.

Moreley shook his head. "Doubtful. He could never hold his liquor at Oxford. Always a pathetic mess." He lowered his voice and said something toward Thornaby and Keldon, smirking all the while. They laughed in response, and the other two gentlemen joined in. Ash, meanwhile, stood stoic. No, not quite stoic. That same ripple passed across his shoulders followed by the tip of his head and the stretching of his neck. And another cough.

Bianca couldn't hear what Moreley said, but was certain it was awful. Yes, he should definitely be the target. It was perhaps a good thing she wasn't shooting.

Moreley took his shot, and the result was slightly closer than the first gentleman. Tealman went next and hit near the edge of the wood. He muttered—probably a curse—under his breath and shook his head as he returned to the table.

Keldon clasped Tealman's bicep. "A good showing. Doubtful you'll be the worst."

He didn't look at Ash, but they all knew whom he was referring to. Bianca doubted anyone else could hear what was being said, but she could. Did they realize? Would they care? How could they treat Ash, who outranked them all, so horribly?

And yet Ash stood there proud and unmoved. Well, almost unmoved. The twitches were coming at intervals now. He cleared his throat several times. She watched as he flexed his hands into fists, loosened them, then repeated the exercise.

Keldon fired and nearly hit the target. The others clapped and cheered. Smugly, Keldon set his firearm on the table and looked to Ash. "Beat that."

"I will." The words shot from his mouth as from one of the pistols in the competition. Ash twitched again, and this time, his arm shuddered. If that happened when he was shooting...

No, it couldn't. It wouldn't. She willed it not to happen. Her father had often told her she had the will of ten men, that she could do anything she set her mind to. In some ways, she'd thought he was patronizing her, but he'd repeated the sentiment several times as he lay ill, and she knew he'd meant it. His belief in her had only increased her determination.

She wanted Ash to know that someone believed in him too. "Of course you will!" she called, smiling broadly in encouragement.

He looked at her, and she felt the weight of his gaze deep in her belly. It held her a moment, trapping her breath in her lungs, then he broke eye contact and walked toward the table.

"Not yet," Keldon said, holding up a hand. "Thornaby first. You always did try to get ahead."

"You mean when I finished school before all of you?" It was a simple statement, and yet so powerful. Bianca resisted the urge to rush over and hug him with glee.

"We weren't in any hurry," Moreley said. "But then, we enjoyed school and had each other."

Keldon sneered. "Aye, that we did. And we still do." There was no mistaking the way in which their words and demeanor excluded Ash. What on earth had he ever done to them? Or were they just cruel?

"Your turn!" Moreley called to Thornaby.

The viscount took his place amidst words of encouragement and a round of applause from the spectators. Because he was the host, presumably. Bianca hoped the gun misfired. Horribly.

It didn't.

The ball wasn't quite as close to the center as Keldon's, but it put him in second place. This was met with more cheers. Finally, it was Ash's turn.

"Sure you don't need to move closer?" Thornaby asked. "None of us would mind. You seem a mite shaky. Wouldn't want your bullet to go wide."

"Egads, no," Moreley said, shaking his head. "Can't have that. I insist you move closer."

Bianca edged toward them because the volume of their conversation was dropping and she didn't want to miss what they said.

"Or maybe he shouldn't shoot at all," Keldon said, looking at Ash with mock pity. Or maybe it was real pity. Bianca couldn't tell, nor did she think it particularly mattered. Either one was rude and wholly unnecessary.

She stalked to them, uncaring how they might react. "Oh stop it, and let him shoot. If he's shaky, it's because you're all behaving like jackasses."

They all gaped at her. Save Ash, who gazed at her in open appreciation.

"Back away, Lady Bianca," Moreley said sharply. "This is no place for you."

Keldon frowned. "Indeed, there's no call to behave in such a fashion. What would your brother say? Come, step away." He moved toward her, his arm outstretched.

"Don't touch her." Ash growled the words, and the air changed. The taunting and mockery gave way to something far more sinister.

Moreley stepped toward Ash, his lip curling. "And what will you do about it?" He glanced toward Keldon as if urging him to continue.

And that was precisely what Keldon did. He took Bianca's elbow and began to steer her away.

The next actions happened so quickly that Bianca had to review them in her mind several times to track how it had all happened.

Though he was farther back from the targets than anyone else had been—behind the table, in fact—Ash lifted his arm and shot at the target, hitting it dead center. Then he dropped the weapon on the table and turned to grab Keldon by the arm.

He dragged Keldon, whose jaw dropped, away from Bianca. "I told you not to touch her, you son of a bitch." Again, the words exploded from his mouth. This was quickly followed by the largest tremor yet. His shoulders twitched, and his neck stretched, thrusting his head to the side. This happened three times in quick succession. Or maybe it was four.

Ash opened his mouth, his face turning a shade of red that outshone his hair, then snapped it closed. He let go of Keldon and, without a look at anyone else, stalked toward the house.

Everyone stared after him. Bianca wanted to follow, to soothe him, to tell him none of them mattered. And to celebrate his victory.

She turned to the target and spoke loudly so that everyone, including Ash, would hear. "He won."

"He cheated," Moreley groused.

Bianca swung her head toward him, anger blazing through her. "How?"

Moreley sniffed. "He didn't stand in the right place."

"You were going to let him move closer! Now you take issue with him shooting farther away?" A growl started low in her throat. "You're just angry because he was better than all of you."

Thornaby straightened his coat. "Never mind. He forfeited with his behavior. I'm sorry you had to witness that, Lady Bianca."

"I'm sorry I had to witness *your* ill behavior."

The viscount's eyes widened, and his mouth opened in surprise. He recovered quickly, his lips forming an easy, false smile. "You witnessed a group of old friends having fun recalling their youth."

Bianca snorted in disgust. "You're awful." And to think she'd wanted to ask him to host the St. Stephen's Day party! She couldn't imagine him wanting to, not with his small mind and petty behavior. It didn't matter—she wasn't going to ask. She'd find another way.

Turning on her heel, she started toward the house. A moment later, Poppy caught up to her. "Wait for me, Bianca!"

Bianca slowed but didn't stop. When Poppy came abreast of her, she said, "I want to leave."

"What happened? We couldn't hear what was going on."

"Thornaby and his friends were behaving horribly toward Ash. He, er, lost his temper—as he should have. In fact, it's a wonder he didn't lose his patience sooner. I would have." She thought of his odd twitches and coughing and of what Poppy had told her earlier about how he'd been before he'd gone to school. Bianca didn't remember him doing any of that before.

They went into the house, and Bianca didn't stop. She continued through on her way to the stairs.

"It looked like you did," Poppy observed. "It appeared as though you were lecturing them."

Bianca glanced at her sister. "So what if I was? They deserve to be lectured. They were horrid to Ash."

"You can't keep calling him Ash," Poppy murmured.

Stopping at the base of the stairs, Bianca turned toward her sister. "Why? I've known him since I was a child. We're friends."

Poppy gave her a beleaguered stare. "You know why. It's not…seemly."

Bianca rolled her eyes and started up the stairs. "I want to go home. After I see *Ash*." She stressed his name on purpose.

When they reached the top, Poppy touched her arm. "You are always looking for trouble. In this case, let it be. At least for a while. The earl appeared upset when he returned to the house. And he shot that gun in a rather unsafe manner. I don't know if you should see him at all."

"He knew precisely what he was doing." And yet, he'd clearly been upset, his body twitching, his face turning red. Ruddy… Her heart ached for him.

"I'm not sure that's an endorsement."

Bianca wouldn't stop her defense of him. "He was being perfectly safe."

"Bianca, just take a few minutes. *Please.*"

Groaning, Bianca scowled but relented. She stalked toward their chamber. Once inside, while Poppy went into the dressing room, she asked her maid to find out where Ash's room was located.

Bianca paced while she awaited Donnelly's return. She wanted Ash to know that she stood with him, that she was going to leave the party before dinner and hoped he would do the same. She also wanted to ask why they treated him so poorly. Would he tell her?

She sensed there was more about his life in London that he hadn't revealed. But then why should he tell her everything? Indeed, why should he tell her *anything*?

Because they were friends. Or they had been. She thought about the way in which he'd reacted to Keldon touching her. He'd fired the pistol at the target almost without looking and hit it square. Then he'd pulled Keldon away from her, and she could have sworn she'd seen malice in his eyes. The emotion had flickered so quickly, she couldn't be sure.

Donnelly entered, interrupting her thoughts. "I'm sorry, my lady, but his lordship has left."

Bianca stared at her. "From Thornhill?"

The maid nodded.

Of course he'd gone. He'd been upset and rightfully so. She planned to go too. "Donnelly, pack our things. We're leaving."

Donnelly blinked in surprise, then nodded. "Yes, my lady."

Poppy came from the dressing room. "Did I hear you say we're leaving?"

"Yes, I told you that outside."

"I didn't think you were serious."

Bianca pursed her lips. "I'm always serious."

"Indeed, you are," Poppy murmured. "Let us go, then. I can't say I'll be sorry, especially after what you told me. Did I hear that Lord Buckleigh has also gone?"

Bianca nodded, her mind already moving five steps beyond their conversation.

"It sounds as if he should have. Good for him."

It was, but now Bianca had to find a way to get to Buck Manor. The entire Christmas season depended on it.

Sometimes it was hell to be a young unmarried lady.

CHAPTER 4

As soon as Ash arrived at Buck Manor, he immersed himself in a hot bath and drank a glass of brandy. Both soothed his mind, even while his soul raged. He'd been a fool to think those men had changed. And yet, *he* had.

His disease had been much worse in his youth. He'd mastered the twitches and vocal interruptions as he'd gotten older, with great effort and because the behaviors had just seemed to lessen. Right around the time he'd started fighting.

"Shall I trim your hair, my lord?" Harris offered.

"Yes, I suppose you should." Ash covered himself in a banyan and sat down for the valet to do his work.

Harris set to work with the shears, working quickly and efficiently, as he did with all things.

"You are astonishingly good at your post," Ash said, looking in the mirror situated over the dressing table in front of him.

"Thank you, my lord. I never could have imagined how much I enjoy being a valet. I never quite fit in as a footman, and I definitely didn't suffice as a groom."

"Is that where you started?" Ash asked. "I hadn't realized."

"At another estate, yes. The other grooms weren't very welcoming. When I left, I learned that I'd been given a position they'd hoped would go to one of their brothers. I believe they ensured I wasn't successful at my position. I have no regret since things have worked out rather well." He smiled as he continued to snip and style Ash's hair.

"What estate was that?"

Harris let out a soft chuckle. "Actually, it was Thornhill."

Ash watched his eyes widen in the mirror, then looked up at Harris behind him. "Did you see any of those men while we were there?"

"I recognized the groom when we arrived, but he didn't behave as if he knew me. I certainly didn't greet him."

Ash could understand that. He also had no trouble believing Thornaby's staff was as cruel as he was. Ash was more glad than ever that he'd promoted Harris. "I know what it's like to feel as though you're a misfit," Ash said.

"I can't imagine that, my lord." Harris finished with the shears and set them on the dressing table. Then he went about brushing the shorn hair from Ash's banyan to the floor.

"It's true." Ash hadn't felt like he fit in until he'd started to box. No one in his pugilism circle had seen the small, terrified boy he'd been at Oxford, the misfit who'd been ridiculed and excluded. They'd only seen the fierce, mostly silent, warrior.

"Hard to think of you, an earl, being an outcast." Harris went to set out Ash's evening clothes.

While Ash had overcome the worst of his disease, he was still different from everyone else. But now he couldn't hide in the shadows. He *was* an earl, but to some extent, he still felt excluded. Because he hadn't been born to the title, and he had much to learn.

Now there were new expectations. He had to speak in the House of Lords and present himself at court and in Society. He also had to wed.

Bee came to his mind, her exuberance, her outspokenness, her staunch loyalty. She accepted him precisely as he was—or so she seemed to. Would she still if she knew he was tainted?

It didn't matter. She'd been quite clear in her desire to remain unwed. Furthermore, she detested London, and since he would spend half the year there, a union with her would be lonely. He'd spent most of his life feeling lonely. When he wed, he hoped it would be to someone with whom he could share everything. Together, they would build a family, and if any of their children suffered his affliction, he would love them and nurture them in ways his father hadn't.

Ash stiffened when he thought of him, how horrified he'd been by Ash's twitches and outbursts, especially when they'd intensified as he'd gotten older. When his father's older brother, the earl, had suggested Ash attend Oxford with Lyndon, Ash's father hadn't been able to agree quickly enough.

Then he'd ignored Ash's pleas to come home. After a few months, Ash had given up and known he was on his own. When his father had died a few years later, just before Ash graduated, Ash had felt relieved. But there was a guilt that came with not mourning one's father.

"My lord?" Thankfully, Harris interrupted Ash's maudlin thoughts.

Ash stood and prepared for dinner.

A short time later, he went down to the dining

room, which was set with just two places as usual. His mother arrived a moment later.

"You *are* home," she said, crossing to him.

Ash kissed her soft cheek and noted the crease in her brow. "Yes." He went to his seat at the head of the table.

"You weren't due until tomorrow. What happened?" The footman helped her into her chair to the left of Ash, and then Ash sat.

He shrugged. "I was bored, and I've far too much to keep me busy here." The estate ledgers were a mess, and there were many issues with the tenants to address, from repairs to cottages to plans for increasing sheep herds.

"I'm sorry to hear it wasn't engaging." Martha Rutledge was the kindest person Ash had ever known. Ash had no living siblings—two older sisters had died in their youth—so his mother focused all her attention, and love, on him. She always worried about her son, so much so that Ash had long ago tried to keep her from fretting. He'd kept his troubles at school from her, as well as his frustration and disappointment with his father.

"I'm sure it was nice to see old friends," she said with a smile as the soup was served.

No it wasn't, with one sparkling exception. "Lady Bianca was there. It was lovely to see her after so many years."

Mother's deep brown eyes lit. "Was she there? I've always liked her. She had such a trying time when her father was ill. I used to see her in town regularly, but I saw her less and less as his sickness progressed."

Ash had kept up on the local happenings somewhat via his mother's letters, but admittedly, he hadn't paid much attention. "The duke was ill for some time?"

Mother nodded while she sipped her soup. "My goodness, for a couple of years at least. And Lady Bianca bore the brunt of it. Her sister is married, of course, but you would have thought Chill would have come home to help."

"He didn't return at all?"

"No, but neither did you." She gave him a slightly vexed look. "I had to come visit you in London."

"I was busy." He focused on his soup.

She exhaled. "I know, and quite successful too."

Yes, he had been. Before Lyndon had died, Ash had been deciding between a potential position with the government or purchasing a commission. Two very different paths, neither of which he'd pursue now.

"Do you miss it?" she asked.

"Sometimes." The boxing mostly, but he'd fashioned a large sack that he hung in a corner of the stable to hit. He had to regularly refill the bag with dirt and straw to keep it firm for his practice, but the concept worked. The sack also didn't hit back. Was that what he missed? Or was it the accolades that came with winning a fight?

"There is plenty to keep me occupied here," he said, hoping to turn the conversation. "Especially with the Christmas season almost upon us. Lady Bianca told me Chill won't be hosting the St. Stephen's Day party this year."

Mother had dipped her spoon in her soup and now dropped it in reaction. "How can he do that? The townspeople will be so disappointed, to say nothing of his retainers, I'm sure."

He'd thought his mother might be upset, but her reaction was greater than he'd anticipated. "It will matter that much?"

She nodded. "Oh yes. It's perhaps the most important day of the year. It's a tradition dating back generations." A deep frown marred her features. "Why isn't he hosting it?"

"I don't know, but Lady Bianca is doing her best to change his mind." Or come up with an alternative. Was she still planning to ask Thornaby? Ash couldn't think she would, not after what had happened earlier. She'd staunchly defended him, turning the tables to become *his* rescuer. But then he'd no idea what might have happened after he left.

"Good," his mother said. "We shouldn't discount her abilities."

That much was true. Still, it did sound as if her brother might be immovable. And then what? Ash didn't want to disappoint the villagers or the people of Hartwood or his mother. Or Bee.

"I'm sure she'll find a way to make it happen." He'd do whatever he could to support her. If she wanted him to. He had no idea what she thought of him after today's outburst.

His gut twisted. He had to stop thinking about that, about the way those men had made him feel. Again.

He'd thought he'd left those emotions behind, that "Ruddy" had died. To think that people judged him for who he'd been and not who he was now was incredibly disheartening.

No, to think that people judged him for an affliction he couldn't control was infuriating.

He took a deep breath to calm his racing pulse. He wouldn't think of them. There was no cause to see them ever again. Except Thornaby in the House of Lords. And potentially all of them at a St. Stephen's Day event, provided Bee was successful.

Of course she would be successful. Even if she wasn't, it was ludicrous to think he wouldn't see them again. How would they all behave after today?

Hopefully, he could simply avoid them. At the party, in London, wherever he might have cause to encounter them.

Or he could beat them all senseless. Yes, that sounded fun.

Ash reached for his wineglass and nearly drained it. He wasn't going to hit anyone. He was better than that. He was better than *them*.

Why, then, did they still have the power to hurt?

～

"Good morning." Bianca sailed into the breakfast room and glanced at her brother. He sat at the table, his plate before him, his nose buried in a newspaper.

He didn't look up. "Why are you home?"

"Good morning, Bianca, how lovely to see you. You're home early from the house party. Is anything amiss?" She glowered at her brother. "It's not difficult to be pleasant."

His gaze lifted slowly from the newspaper and fixed on her with cool irritation. "Good morning, Bianca. Why are you home early from the house party?"

His second attempt was laced with sarcasm, but she'd take it. "Because it was dreadful." She went to the sideboard and served up her plate before taking a seat opposite her brother at the table.

She didn't really want to get into the specifics—the horrid way in which Ash had been treated. "The new Earl of Buckleigh was there. It was wonderful to see him again."

Calder had looked back down at the paper and

now he glanced up, his brow creasing. "Lyndon's cousin?"

"Yes. Ash," she said, picking up a piece of toast.

The furrow in his brow deepened as he regarded her. "'Ash'? That sounds awfully familiar."

"I knew him when we were children. I always called him Ash. 'Buckleigh' or 'my lord' is just odd."

"It's also proper." His tone took on an edge of condescension. "He, however, is not. I'd prefer you stay away from him."

Bianca's jaw froze as she chewed her toast. She took a drink of tea to wash it down. "How on earth is Ash not proper?"

"Stop calling him that. He had a reputation in certain circles in London."

The hair on the back of her neck stood up. "What sort of reputation?"

"A dangerous one." He gave her a pointed stare. "He was a pugilist. I saw him fight a few times, and he's brutal. Definitely not the sort of man with whom my sister should associate, let alone be familiar with." He scoffed as he returned his attention to the newspaper and his breakfast.

Bianca stared at the window that looked out over the rolling parkland of the estate. A sloping hill met a stand of bare-branched trees beneath the dove-gray sky. It looked cold and forbidding, not at all like the fire-haired gentleman who'd made her laugh just yesterday.

"I can't believe that's true." She shook her head and cut a bite of ham.

"What, that he's a pugilist or a particularly fierce one?" Calder lifted a shoulder. "Both are true. As I said, I saw him fight. Or do you doubt me?" He pierced her with his frigid stare, challenging her to cross him.

"I don't doubt you think it was him, but I just

can't see it." Ash had always been kinder than most everyone. Together, they'd saved animals and insects and talked about how they wanted all the women and children at the Institution for Impoverished Women in Hartwell to have a warm hearth and a full belly. To that end, Bianca had always done her best to support Hartwell House, which was the name everyone called it. Did Ash feel the same as he had in their youth, or had London corrupted him somehow?

She recalled his evasiveness when discussing his time there and the sensation she'd had that he'd left something out. She also thought of how quickly and savagely he'd shot the pistol, hitting the target with almost no effort. Then there was the malice and fury in his eyes. The emotions had been well earned, but was there more buried within him?

"Whether you see it or not, it's true, and I don't want you associating with him. He's certainly not marriage material—not for you, anyway—and that's where your mind should be. Thornaby would be a good match."

She couldn't keep from snorting in disgust. "Thornaby is a bully. He'd be a good match for a simpleton with no sympathy or capacity to care for others. And what's more, my mind is on St. Stephen's Day and what I shall do if you insist on not hosting the party."

Calder looked at her sharply. "There will be no party. Not here."

She stared at him a long moment, trying to find the caring brother she'd grown up with. "You really mean it, don't you?"

"I don't say things I don't mean." He shifted his attention back to the newspaper.

"Then I shall have to find another way. I refuse

to disappoint the people of Hartwood and Hartwell."

"If you think a party has the means to keep from disappointing people, you've a great deal to learn. Life is more than parties and celebrations and tradition."

At least he knew tradition was part of it. But he also didn't seem to care. "Yes, life is more than that," she said softly. "It's also family and duty and loyalty and love."

He glanced toward her briefly, his lips pressed into a flat line. "Duty—at least we agree on that. Consider Thornaby, or, if you'd rather, I'll come up with a list of potential suitors. You should have a few in mind when you get to London for the Season."

"I'm not going to London for the Season." She'd told him that a dozen times, and he never seemed to listen.

"Of course you are."

She sweetly tossed his words back at him. "I don't say things I don't mean. I'm not going to London."

His gaze lifted at a glacial pace. His stare was so cold, so unfathomable, that she imagined he'd scare just about anyone with it. Not her, however. "It isn't up for debate." His lips barely moved. Was he actually carved from ice?

"I would agree. I'm not going, and that's final." She stood from the table, having lost her appetite. "I am, however, going to Poppy's. Perhaps it's warmer there."

"You *are* going to London, and *that's* final." He looked back down at the newspaper. "I doubt it's warmer at Poppy's. She's only seven miles away. It looks like it may snow, which means you'll have to stay the night. Prepare accordingly." He picked up the newspaper and held it up, blocking his face from her.

Apparently, she was dismissed.

A combination of frustration and agitation propelled her from the breakfast room. Perhaps she would ask Poppy if she could move in with her and her husband. They wouldn't mind.

But she couldn't. Poppy and Gabriel had their own troubles, and Bianca didn't think she could live with the tension. With Calder, she could mostly avoid him. However, she couldn't avoid her sister, especially when she suffered such heartache… In fact, that was maybe another reason Bianca should consider at least staying there for a period of time. Such as for the entire Christmas season…

Well, she would discuss it with Poppy next time she saw her. That wasn't, however, going to be today. She had another destination in mind.

Energized, Bianca flew up the stairs to "prepare," as Calder had put it. She wanted to get on the road within the hour, and she would pray it wouldn't snow.

A devilish grin sprouted across her lips, unbidden. Actually, she might not pray that hard.

CHAPTER 5

*T*he coach slowed in front of Buck Manor. With a tall Palladian façade and sprawling wings to the east and west, the house commanded respect and awe. It wasn't as large as Hartwood, but it was larger than Poppy's home, Darlington Abbey.

Thinking of her sister only reminded Bianca that she'd lied to the coachman upon leaving Hartwood. She'd had him stop the coach after the first two miles, when it had become necessary to change course, and told him of her change in destination. He'd seemed hesitant at first, but that was largely because he was concerned it would snow.

Both he and Calder had proved right. The snow, falling softly at first, was now coming down in earnest. As Bianca stepped out of the coach, she tilted her head up and was promptly rewarded with a snowflake landing on her nose.

She smiled and started toward the house. Donnelly, who'd accompanied her, followed.

"My lady?" the coachman said, causing her to stop and turn. Donnelly paused with her, then stepped out of Bianca's line of sight so she could see the coachman.

"Yes?" Bianca asked.

"Will this be a quick visit?" He glanced up at the sky.

"It won't be terribly long, but why don't you take the horses to the stables where they will be warmer?"

He nodded and returned to the vehicle while Bianca continued toward the house. They didn't reach the door before it opened. The butler ushered them inside.

"Welcome to Buck Manor," he said. "May I take your cloak?"

Bianca pivoted and unclasped the outer garment. "Thank you. Please let his lordship know that Lady Bianca is here to see him. Can my maid warm up somewhere and perhaps have a cup of tea?"

The butler removed her cloak, and she handed him her gloves and hat. "Of course, my lady. I'll see to it. May I show you to the drawing room?"

"That would be lovely. I hope there's a fire."

He smiled as he handed her things off to a footman. "Indeed there is." He looked toward the footman and murmured, "Please see her ladyship's maid to the downstairs parlor."

Bianca nodded at Donnelly before following the butler from the hall into a large reception room decorated in greens and golds. She went directly to the massive fireplace and warmed her hands before the crackling flames.

Would Ash mind that she'd come? Would he ask her to leave? She flicked a glance toward the windows, where she could see the snow was falling at an even greater pace. Could she leave even if he wanted her to?

"Bee?" Ash's voice carried through the large drawing room, sending a surprising dash of heat up her spine. Surprising because her back was away from the fireplace.

And probably she didn't want to consider that Ash was the source.

Turning, she greeted him with a smile. "I hope you don't mind that I've come."

"Not at all." He seemed genuinely happy to see her, coming forward with a welcoming grin. "I'm surprised. And delighted." He looked around the room. "It's just you?"

"Yes. I told Calder I was visiting Poppy. He's being a pain in my—" She inhaled quickly and blew the breath back out. "Never mind. I plan to go to Poppy's after this. Provided the weather isn't too bad." She looked toward the window again.

"It doesn't look good," Ash said. "Perhaps we should be brief."

"That's what my coachman suggested. I can try." Only she didn't want to. Now that she was here, she wanted to stay. No, if she were honest, she'd hoped it would snow so that she would *have* to stay. They had much to discuss—the St. Stephen's Day party first and foremost. Also his reputation and whether he was a brutal, merciless pugilist. She brought up none of those things. Instead, she asked, "Is your mother here?"

"Yes. I already asked Cornelius to fetch her."

"Wonderful." Bianca was looking forward to seeing her. But first, she supposed she ought to broach what had happened the day before at Thornhill. "I wanted to talk to you about yesterday."

He stiffened, and the air between them shifted as if a wall had sprung up. "There's nothing to discuss. I apologize for leaving without bidding you farewell."

She waved her hand. "That's the least of my

concerns. Actually, I have no concern about that at all." That wasn't precisely true. She'd felt disappointed upon learning he'd gone. "I wanted you to know that I found the behavior of Thornaby and the others reprehensible. It was my privilege to speak up for you."

"Thank you." His voice was soft but his features hard. He gazed at the window instead of at her.

Bianca moved toward him, eager to unwrap the secrets enveloping him. "Has it always been like that with them?"

"Yes, not that I've seen them in a very long time." He shook his head and finally turned his attention to her. "Anyway, it hardly signifies. I don't plan on spending time with them in the future."

"Me neither," she said with great satisfaction and a supportive smile. "May I ask why they call you Ruddy?"

Unfortunately, she wasn't to receive an answer because his mother arrived. Mrs. Rutledge entered with a swish of lavender skirts and a broad smile. "Lady Bianca!"

She came to Bianca, and they embraced warmly. "How lovely to see you, Mrs. Rutledge. I see becoming the mother to an earl agrees with you."

She laughed. "Being Ashton's mother has always agreed with me." She looked at him with pride and love, and Bianca felt a twinge of regret. She had no parents left to look at her like that, and her brother certainly wasn't going to bestow that sort of care or affection on her.

"Come, let us sit," Mrs. Rutledge said, gesturing toward the seating area nestled close to the fire. She looked outside and shuddered. "What an awful day to be out."

"It wasn't snowing when I left," Bianca said,

lowering herself to the dark green settee. "I was on my way to my sister's, but I daresay I may be stranded here."

Mrs. Rutledge took an adjacent chair. "Oh, I think you might be. That snow is starting to pile up."

Ash sat down next to Bianca. Well, not *next* to her—a good foot separated them.

"I do love snow," Bianca said on a sigh. "I may have to go out and traipse through it if it's thick enough."

"Take Ashton with you. He always adored the snow. Did you miss it in London, dear?"

"It snowed in London," he said. "Perhaps not as much, but enough to satisfy my desire."

Something about those three words sent another lick of heat up Bianca's spine.

The butler, Cornelius, arrived with a tray. He set out a plate of cake and biscuits along with a pot of tea and three cups. Mrs. Rutledge said she would pour, recalling exactly how Bianca preferred her tea. The same as Ash—just a splash of cream and a dash of sugar.

When the butler retreated, Ash's mother asked, "What prompted you to stop at Buck Manor today?"

Ash responded before Bianca could. "She came to talk about the St. Stephen's Day party."

Bianca regarded him closely. He'd been careful to answer and had provided a reason she hadn't even brought up. Did he not want his mother to know about yesterday? More secrets. Which only made her more determined to unravel them. To unravel *him*.

In fact, she *had* come to talk about the party, so in that sense, she and Ash were of a mind. "Yes, I was hoping you and Ash might have some thoughts about the party. Did Ash tell you that my brother is refusing to host it?"

Mrs. Rutledge nodded somberly before sipping her tea. "He did, and I'm sorry to hear it. Is there no persuading him?"

"I'm afraid he's proving quite intractable." Bianca picked up her cup with a grimace. "I'm resolved to find an alternate solution. Not having the party is simply not an option. I will not let the people of Hartwell and Hartwood down."

"You've such a kind and generous heart," Mrs. Rutledge said. "But then I've always known that." She looked to her son. "Did you know that Lady Bianca has worked tirelessly at Hartwell House to ensure the residents have proper clothing, food, and opportunity? She even teaches the children to read."

"When I can," Bianca said, feeling a trifle embarrassed for perhaps the first time ever. She busied herself with eating a biscuit.

"That does not surprise me," Ash said with soft appreciation. "We always planned to rescue everyone there and make sure they had jobs and homes and families."

Her eyes met his, and the heat she'd felt along her spine spread through her. "We did indeed." After a moment, she pulled her gaze from his and looked to his mother. "That's why it's so important to me to ensure there is a St. Stephen's Day celebration. If nothing else, there must be a celebration for the women and children at Hartwell House. Christmas should be a joyous time, with plenty for everyone."

"I wonder…" Mrs. Rutledge tipped her head to the side and looked into the fire. "I know Shield's End isn't terribly large, but much of the festivities has always happened outside, weather permitting.

We could use the house as the kitchen and repository for all the food and supplies."

Bianca clasped her hands together. Using Ash's childhood home was an excellent solution. "What a wonderful idea!"

"See, there's a reason we didn't sell it," Ash said, smiling.

His mother chuckled. "I wanted to, but you said we should wait. It's a credit to your forethought. Though how you could have predicted this, I'm not sure."

"I didn't. I was just reluctant to let it go." His cheeks turned a faint pink as he sipped his tea.

Bianca understood the sentiment. There was something very special about tradition and roots and the things—both tangible and not—that made one's life special and beloved. "Just as I refuse to let the St. Stephen's Day party die."

"Precisely," Mrs. Rutledge said. "So we'll host it at Shield's End." She rubbed her hands together, grinning. "I can't wait to get started. There's so much to do in the next month!"

The woman's enthusiasm was infectious, not that Bianca needed any motivation to be excited about this plan. "I will write to all the people who typically support the party with food and drink." She thought of Thornaby and his friends. Asking them was out of the question. And Calder had been plain: he would do nothing. "Now that I think of it, I'm not sure whom to ask." She looked toward Ash, who nodded almost imperceptibly.

"I'll take care of it," he said.

"All the food and drink?" his mother asked with grave surprise. "That's an enormous undertaking. There are plenty of people in the area who can—and should—help."

Ash stood abruptly and went to the window. "I

don't think you'll be going anywhere, Bee. The snow is accumulating, and your carriage will be trapped before it leaves my drive."

Pity. Bianca's insides somersaulted. "I have my maid and was prepared to stay with Poppy, so it's no inconvenience to stay here. I hope it's not an imposition."

He turned and met her gaze. "Not at all. I'll have Cornelius prepare you a room. Dinner is at seven. Now, if you'll excuse me, I've some correspondence to finish." He bowed to them and left.

Bianca realized he'd done everything possible to avoid discussing the prospect of asking others to help with the party. It was evident he didn't want his mother to know about the enmity between him and the other gentlemen in the area.

Gentlemen? They weren't gentlemen, they were cads.

"As to whom you should ask for help," Mrs. Rutledge said after nibbling a cake. "I recall Viscount Thornaby always supported the event, as did Keldon. I'm sure there are others. Regardless of what Ashton says, it's not right that he shoulder the entire burden."

Bianca agreed, but she also respected his desire not to ask for help. His pride was important. Furthermore, she wasn't sure those bullies would provide assistance if Ash was at the center of it. Would they, however, if she asked?

It didn't matter. She didn't want to ask them. She'd go back to Calder and plead with him to at least provide food and ale. He couldn't say no.

He could, and he very likely would. She frowned into her teacup before taking a sip of the now tepid liquid.

"I'd be happy to help with the correspondence," Mrs. Rutledge offered.

"I'll start with my sister," Bianca said quickly. In the past, the occupants and some of the household staff of Hartwood and Darlington Abbey did the bulk of the work. Other estates in the area, such as Buck Manor and Thornhill, would also help. They'd just have to make do without Thornaby and his friends. She gave Ash's mother a bright smile. "You focus on preparing Shield's End."

Mrs. Rutledge nodded. "I'm sure we can find enough people willing to help. I'm so sorry to hear your brother isn't willing to host the party. I own I'm surprised given how important this event has always been to your family."

"No one was more surprised than me." Bianca wondered if she'd ever learn what was going on in her brother's head. She feared she never would. She also feared he was lost to them, that the Calder they'd known and loved was gone forever. If she only knew why, perhaps there was a way they could bring him back.

Cornelius entered the drawing room and looked to Bianca. "If you're ready, my lady, I'd be happy to show you to your room."

Bianca stood. "Thank you, yes."

Mrs. Rutledge also got to her feet. She gave Bianca another quick hug. Then she held her hands as she spoke. "I'm so pleased you've come. I daresay it's not altogether proper, but I am here to act as chaperone." She waggled her brows. "Do I need to act as chaperone? I don't know that my son is looking for a countess yet, but I can think of no one better."

Oh dear. Bianca wasn't remotely interested in marriage. Not to Ash. Not to anyone.

And yet, the thought of being *Ash's* countess provoked a captivating thrill...

Bianca squeezed Mrs. Rutledge's hands before

letting them go. "Ash and I are old friends. We don't need a chaperone except that propriety demands one." Bianca rolled her eyes. "Not that it matters out here." This was yet another reason she had no interest in a London Season. Society and its ridiculous rules. She would feel so constrained, so *trapped*.

"Hopefully, your sister won't be worried when you don't arrive," Mrs. Rutledge said.

"She'll realize the weather is to blame. With luck, the snow will stop soon or overnight, and I'll be able to travel tomorrow."

Or not. Bianca could think of nothing better than spending a day in the snow with Ash. She'd pelt him with snowballs, and they could take a ride so they could race, and she would beat him again.

Only maybe she'd let him win this time. Except she suspected he let her win last time. Her pulse quickened at the prospect. Either way, it would be a wonderful way to spend the day.

Goodness, maybe they needed a chaperone after all.

CHAPTER 6

*A*sh managed to ensure the conversation at dinner had veered quite clear of the St. Stephen's Day party. Instead, they focused on stories of their youth. He credited Bianca with supporting his intent to avoid discussing the party—specifically asking people to help. She understood him like no one ever had.

It was, in a word, enthralling.

The snow had continued into the evening, finally tapering off while they'd dined. Now it was nearly midnight, and the house was dark and quiet. He crept downstairs with the plan of stealing outside to see if the snow had started again or if the sky had cleared.

Carrying a lantern, he walked through the hall toward the back of the house to the terrace. A flash of blue from the library drew him to a stop. A candelabrum on a table inside illuminated Bianca. She stood near the flickering light, her head bent as she cradled a book in her hand.

Ash simply stood there and watched her a moment. Her dark hair hung in a loose plait over her shoulder, the end curling against the swell of her breast. Outlined beneath the Egyptian blue of her dressing gown, her body beckoned him—the elegant slope of her shoulder, the gentle indentation of her waist, the alluring curve of her hip. Good God, when had he become so drawn to her?

Her gaze lifted from the book and turned toward him, perhaps sensing his presence. Smiling, she snapped the book closed. "Ash."

He walked into the library as if he were pulled by a magnet. "I wasn't expecting to find you here."

"What were you expecting to find?"

"Nothing, really. I was on my way outside to see if the snow had started again or if it was truly finished."

She quickly set the book on a table and moved to stand before him, her gaze eager. "I'll come with you."

He offered her his arm, and as her warm hand curled around him, he was painfully aware that they were both barely dressed—she in a dressing gown and he in a banyan over his shirt and a pair of breeches. This was wholly improper, and he didn't give a damn.

This was Bee. They'd known each other forever, it seemed. Friends since childhood. Yet, this was something more. He wondered if she felt it too.

He guided her out to the terrace where the snow was maybe three inches deep. They barely stepped outside, staying clear of the snow.

She looked up into the ink-dark sky. "It *is* snowing."

Surveying the white terrace, she lifted the hem of her gown and waded into the snow. "Ooh, it's cold and wet." She lifted a careless shoulder before tipping her head back.

Light, soft flakes landed on her upturned face. He held up the lantern to see the graceful planes of her cheekbones, the bright, dazzling sparkle of her blue eyes. He'd never seen anything more beautiful. He moved toward her and wiped a snowflake from her cheek.

She brought her head down to look at him, her lips parted in joy. He brought his finger to his mouth and licked the snowflake from the pad.

Her gaze fixed on his mouth, and the desire that had been swirling inside him all day swelled to a crescendo, hardening his cock and making his breath come short.

"We always tried to catch the snowflakes." She tipped her head back and closed her eyes, then stuck out her tongue.

What was beautiful was now also incredibly erotic. Ash told himself to go inside, to tell her she should return to her chamber. But he did neither. He stared at her mouth and thought of her tongue doing unspeakable things. He thought of kissing her beneath the snowy sky.

He didn't do that either.

She caught a snowflake and drew her tongue back between her lips. Her eyes opened, and it was as if he could see straight into her soul—a bright beacon that was now emblazoned in his memory. He wondered if she could have been a light in the darkness at Oxford. He would never know.

Soft, bliss-filled laughter slipped from her mouth. "Too bad it's dark, or I would bombard you with snowballs."

"Not if I bombarded you first."

She gave him a saucy stare. "Is that a challenge?"

"It might be, but it will require boots and appropriate outerwear—and daylight."

She exhaled with regret. "And a hot bath when we're finished."

Hell, now he was thinking of her nude in a bath,

steam rising from the water. He nearly groaned with want. Again he wondered how his childhood friend had suddenly become the object of his greatest desire.

Ash coughed and worked to suppress the shudder that threatened to crane his neck and roll his shoulders. "If you're suggesting we engage in a snowball fight and then take a hot bath, I'll have to remind you that propriety would frown upon it."

"I didn't mean together." A faint pink stained her cheeks, but he couldn't know if it was because of their flirtation or the cold temperature. "But remember that propriety is the least of my concerns." She twirled about in the snow, her arms out wide. Flakes clung to her dark hair, making her look like a winter princess.

"Were you really on your way to your sister's?" he asked.

She stopped and dropped her arms to her sides. "Yes, but I knew it was possible I might be stranded here because of the weather."

"And you came here just to talk with me about…yesterday." He didn't really want to bring it up again, and yet he couldn't seem to stop himself. He wanted to know why she was *really* here.

He wanted to know if there was something blossoming between them. No, he knew there was for him. He needed to know if the sensation was present for her too.

"Not just for that, no." Her words prompted his pulse to quicken. "As I said, Calder was being insufferable, so I was anxious to be anywhere but Hartwood. I also wanted to speak with you about St. Stephen's Day—I'm so glad we resolved that."

Mostly. He still didn't want to involve Thornaby or anyone else.

She stepped toward him until there was barely

any space between them. "I know you don't want Thornaby or Keldon or any of the others to help. I don't either. I also realize you don't want your mother to know you don't want them involved."

She was incredibly perceptive. And caring. He suddenly acknowledged there had been a dreadful weight on his chest for as long as he could remember. He noticed its presence in this moment because it lightened, and he felt...free. A gentle twitch moved across his shoulders.

The snow was clinging to her brows now, and a shiver jolted her frame.

"Let's go inside." He swept his arm around her waist and ushered her back into the house.

She shuddered, sending snow flying from her dressing gown and her hair. "I didn't realize how cold it was. You distracted me." Her gaze met his, her brow arching. "You also changed the subject. Again."

He laughed softly. "Only because I didn't want you to freeze. You need to get out of that wet dressing gown." He placed his hand against the small of her back. The silk of her gown was damp, and he pulled his hand away. Not because he didn't want to get wet, but because he didn't want to press the cold material against her skin.

"You can touch me." With her words and the impassioned look in her eyes, a different weight settled into him. One that was welcome with its heat and intensity.

He put his hand lightly against her as he guided her toward the stairs. "I don't want you to catch cold."

"I will disrobe as soon as I get upstairs. Will that suffice?" She gave him a heated stare, and he wasn't sure if she was being playful or serious. Did it matter? His body burned hotter at the thought of her removing her gown…

They started up the stairs. "Bee, are you flirting with me?"

"Probably." Her voice had dipped to a lower timbre, one he felt in his bones. "It's just…" They weren't quite to the top of the stairs, but she stopped and turned toward him. "I was so angry yesterday. I wanted you to know that." She searched his face, her lips slightly parted, her chest rising and falling with her breath.

He sensed there was more. "What else did you want me to know?"

"Actually, it's what *I'd* like to know. You said London was a long story, and then you prevaricated—don't pretend you didn't." Her tone was scolding, but with an underlying warmth. "My brother told me you were a pugilist." She blinked. "Is that true?"

He felt his heart beat in his neck along with a rush of excitement. The combination of thrill and trepidation when something so guarded was about to be revealed. "It is."

Her eyes widened slightly with surprise, and her lips parted as she stared at him for a moment. Her reaction was troubling.

"That bothers you," he said.

"I don't know if it does," she admitted, sounding tense. "My brother said you were dangerous, that I should stay away from you."

"I take it he doesn't know you're here?" She shook her head, and he couldn't help a short chuckle. "You really don't care about propriety, do you?"

She shook her head again. Then she took his hand. "I didn't think you could be dangerous—not the Ash I knew. But then you shot that pistol, and you looked so—"

"Angry." That word didn't remotely encompass the emotion he'd felt. The rage, the pain, feelings he'd thought long buried. He gripped her hand more tightly. "I'm not dangerous. Not to you."

He was too aware that they were standing on the stairs, not that he expected anyone to be about. He squeezed her hand and led her up to the landing. Without speaking, he took her to the left toward his private apartments. A few moments later, he ushered her into his outer sitting room, where a low fire burned.

Positioning her in front of the fire, he said, "Stand there and don't move."

Her brows climbed her forehead, but there was humor in her gaze. She nodded mutely and moved closer to the warmth.

Satisfied she would not catch cold, he went to the sideboard, where he poured two glasses of brandy. He returned to her and offered the tumbler. "This will warm you from the inside."

Lurid images of other ways he could warm her from the inside filled his mind. Why had he brought her here of all places?

So he could explain.

He sipped the brandy, and she did the same.

She swirled the amber liquid in the glass. "French brandy?"

"Lyndon had a fair supply of it. Smuggled, I'm sure." He took another sip to steady his nerves and keep from arching his neck. "I've never talked to anyone about why I fought."

Pivoting, she faced him in front of the fire. "Fought as in the past? You don't fight anymore?"

He turned to her, shaking his head. "Not since

Lyndon died. It seemed I should stop doing that if I am to be the earl."

"Do you miss it?"

"Nearly every day." A weak smile surfaced from within him, conjured by his regret. "Not as much as before—the earldom keeps me very busy. Before that, I had my work and fighting."

"Nothing else?"

"No. I needed both those things to overcome my...affliction."

The space between her brows gathered. She took a step toward him. "What affliction?"

"Surely you've noticed it. The way I twitch, the vocalizations?"

She nodded. "My sister mentioned it—she recalls you doing that before you went to school, but I don't."

"You were very young, not quite ten, I believe."

"Yes, but you visited, and although I didn't see you very often, I still don't remember you doing those things." She frowned. "What causes it?"

"I don't know. I've always been that way. It grew more troublesome as I started to mature." The twitches could be almost constant, and the vocalizations, including words and phrases he would never voluntarily say aloud, could happen at any moment. "At school, it was horrible."

"Thornaby and the others taunted you for it," she said flatly.

"Lyndon was the worst. When we had lessons together in our youth, he often mocked my efforts —the symptoms have always displayed when I am nervous or tense." He glanced from her toward the fire. "Or afraid." Conquering his fear through fighting had been his primary goal after Oxford. Admitting it aloud to another person was, he supposed, another victory.

"Is that why they called you Ruddy?" she asked.

"Because my face would grow red, both from embarrassment and my efforts to control myself."

"You seem to be in control now."

"Mostly." He tipped his head to the side, and a small smile flitted across his lips. "Like that. It seems innocuous, but I can't control it."

She reached up and cupped her hand against his jaw. "How does it feel?" The question was soft and rife with concern as well as a genuine need to understand.

"I don't know that I can explain it. When I was younger, it was as if I was standing outside myself watching it happen to someone else. Now, it's simply who I am. Along with my red hair—that's the other reason they called me Ruddy. And my name, Rutledge."

She slipped her hand back behind his ear and ran her fingers through his thick strands. "I have always adored your hair. I wanted it for myself. It's so vivid and full of fire and energy."

Anticipation continued to build inside him. "Like you." The words tumbled from his mouth, not that he would have stopped them. If he was losing control where she was concerned, he wasn't sure he wanted to rein himself in.

But he should.

"Yes," she whispered. "Your hair is how I feel inside—it isn't fair that it belongs to you."

He grinned, utterly charmed by this woman. And yes, she was very much a woman and not the girl from his youth. "Bee—Bianca—I'm going to kiss you unless you tell me not to."

She stared up at him, then dropped her hand from his hair. Turning her head, she set her glass atop the mantelpiece before returning her gaze to his. Her lips didn't part, and the look she gave him overflowed with expectation. With invitation.

Ash set his unfinished brandy next to hers. He cupped his hands against her cheeks and moved closer until their chests touched. "Last chance," he murmured just before his lips grazed hers.

Her palms flattened against his chest, her heat seeping into him through the damp of his banyan. He took that as encouragement and pressed his mouth to hers. She moved beneath him, tentative at first. He went slow, both to give her time to adjust and to decide if she wanted to stop.

Then her fingers curled into the silk of his banyan, and she leaned into him. So much for going slow. Still, he kept control. He tipped his head to the side—completely on purpose this time —and opened his mouth against hers. Gently, he slid his tongue along her lower lip.

"Open," he whispered against her.

She parted her lips, and he slipped his tongue inside. Again, her fingers dug into him, this time the tips pressing into his flesh through the fabric. Her tongue moved against his, her mouth blooming beneath his, and the concert between them began.

The song lifted his soul, and he cradled her nape with one hand while he trailed the other down her back and pressed against her lower spine. He withdrew from her mouth only to begin again from a new angle so he could learn every part of her. She met him eagerly, greedily, her hands clutching at his neck, her body straining against his.

He moved his hand lower to her backside and pulled her flush against his erection. A low groan rumbled in his chest, and she pulled away.

What am I doing?

This was Bee. Not some London trollop. He stepped back and lifted his hand to his mouth, horrified. "I'm so sorry."

She glared at him, and he'd never felt worse in his life.

Then she untied the sash at her waist and let her dressing gown fall to the floor. Beneath the garment, she wore only a thin chemise, through which he could see every curve and slope of her body.

His mouth went utterly dry, and he had to know if this was all in his mind. "What are you doing?"

"Encouraging you not to stop. Is it working?"

Wait, she didn't want him to stop?

He blinked at her, trying to make sense of what was happening—between them and within himself. He'd never wanted anything more than he wanted Bianca.

Blowing out an exasperated breath, she drew her chemise over her head and kicked her slippers from her feet. "How about now? Please tell me this is enough to tempt you, because I can't take anything else off. I suppose I can try seduction, but I haven't the faintest idea what to do—"

He would never know if she meant to say anything else because he swept her up against his chest and kissed her fiercely. It was some minutes later before he came up for a breath.

He stared down into her eyes. "I am seduced."

CHAPTER 7

Glee mixed with excitement and anticipation as Bianca clutched his neck. This was not at all what she'd envisioned when she'd decided to come here today, and yet she couldn't say she was surprised. It felt—to her, at least—like the inevitable conclusion to their acquaintance. As if their childhood had been a precursor to this so that they would have a shared background that would bind them together as nothing else could.

Or maybe it was just that when he kissed her, she felt as though she was going to melt into a puddle. Not *just* when he kissed her. The way he looked at her. The way he spoke to her. The way he valued who she was and how she lived her life. No one else made her feel so…right.

"Show me what to do," she whispered.

His warm brown eyes held hers. "You're certain?"

She nodded. "Never more."

One of his auburn brows arched high on his forehead with a hint of humor. "You have always been a woman of conviction." He lifted her and carried her through a doorway.

Into his bedchamber. The room was large, but the four-poster bed sat in a place of prominence on a raised dais against the wall opposite the fireplace. Heavy dark blue drapes edged with gold hung about the bed, and the bedclothes were even more opulent—rich, deep blues and golds swirling on the coverlet.

"It's a bit ostentatious for my taste," he said, setting her down. "However, I've other things I prefer to spend money on. Such as hosting a St. Stephen's Day party."

She came up on her knees and put her arms around his neck. "Oh, Ash. You are so very wonderful."

Their lips met once more, and she surrendered to his kiss. No, not surrendered, for she was an equal instigator. In fact, it seemed she could do more to further her cause.

She slid her hands into the opening of his banyan and pushed it from his shoulders. There was a sash, she recalled, but he was already undoing it, and the garment slid to the floor.

Dipping her gaze to his shirt and breeches, she frowned slightly. "You are wearing far more clothes than me."

"An unlikely situation since women are typically far more clothed than men. However, we can easily rectify the situation."

"Yes, please." She found the hem of his shirt, which was loose from his breeches, and pulled the garment over his head. He provided assistance, casting it away as soon as he could.

She studied his bare chest in the firelight. "Here are your freckles." A light smattering of pale brown spots dotted his upper chest. "I was afraid they'd disappeared."

"I was glad when they did."

"I was thinking that I missed them." She ran her fingers over his flesh, glorying in the heat and firmness of him. Then she dipped her head and kissed the largest freckle she could find.

"*Bee*."

"You're still wearing breeches."

She closed her eyes and kissed upward, along his sternum and neck. He cast his head back as she felt him working open his fall. A moment later, they were gone from him, or at least they sounded like they were.

Bianca skimmed her hands down his chest, relishing the ripples of his ribs and abdominal muscles, in search of his waistband. There was no garment to block her passage. There was, however, his cock.

Her hands stilled, and she pulled back slightly, looking down at his sex. She'd never seen a man like this in person. Oh, she'd seen drawings—hidden in the bottom shelf of the library at Hartwood—but nothing could compare to this. To Ash.

"Do you wish to stop?" he asked. The words were so lovely, like a verbal caress.

She lifted her gaze to his and shook her head. "No."

"I may keep asking, in case you change your mind."

"I won't." She couldn't imagine stopping now. She wanted this—she wanted *him*. "But that you would accept that is lovely."

"Of course I would. I don't want you to regret this."

"I couldn't. Now, tell me how to seduce you."

He laughed softly. "As I said, I am already seduced. You, on the other hand, require my attention." He brought his hand to her breast, sliding it up beneath and lifting the weight of her.

The sensation was simple but incredibly deca-
dent. She'd never imagined she could feel such desire. It started where he touched her and spread
outward, spiraling down through her belly and
pooling between her legs. When he'd first kissed
her, a spark had lit there, and now he kindled the
flames, stoking a fire within her that begged to
burn.

His hand closed over her, and he captured her
lips once more. She kissed him back, but her focus
was fixed on him touching her breast. He stroked
her gently, drawing his fingers over her nipple. It
was both too much and not enough.

She pressed into him, offering all that he could
possibly take. He left her mouth, his lips blazing a
path down her neck and across her collarbone.
Pushing her breast up, he held her captive to his
mouth. And then he sucked.

The sensation between her legs intensified. She
felt like an utter wanton, desperate for him to
touch her there to ease the ache growing inside
her. She clamped her legs together, seeking something to satisfy her need.

His free hand skimmed along her belly and out
to her waist, then lower to her hip. His touch was
soft and subtle, but she was aware of every graze of
his fingers and brush of his palm. He curled his
hand behind her, stroking the curve of her
backside.

The flesh between her legs began to throb.
"Touch me."

He dragged his hand back along her hip and
down her thigh, coasting inward as he went.
"Here?" he murmured just before he stroked
her sex.

Oh yes, but much, much more. "You're teasing
me."

He lifted his head and gave her a sultry smile. "That's part of sex. The teasing, the anticipation." He skimmed his fingers over her, a light caress designed to torture her, she was certain.

"If you are trying to heighten my awareness, I should tell you that I am keenly aware in ways I have never been before. I do think I may die if you don't touch me."

"We wouldn't want that." His thumb found the top of her sex, and he pressed. "I believe this right here is what you want me to touch."

She gasped as lights danced before her eyes. Every sensation seemed to gather and tighten in that very spot. "*Yes.*"

"And if I continue to do so, your desire will climb." He stroked his thumb and fingers over her, doing exactly as he said. "If I go faster, the pleasure will build until you're unable to stand another moment."

Everything he described was true. Her legs felt weak, and she began to crumble. He eased her back on the bed until she lay before him. She wanted to watch him, to share this with him, but as her body began to shudder, her eyes closed.

"Now come for me, Bee." He moved his fingers faster, then slid one inside her. She *couldn't* stand another moment. Every one of her muscles was pulled tight as her body gathered into a storm. She wasn't sure what he was doing, just that pleasure was raining down on her. It was a torrent of lightning and thunder that broke suddenly free into a bright and roaring crescendo.

"Shhh," he whispered against her ear.

Vaguely, she became aware of his body against hers, of his hand stroking her sex, calming her after the storm. She opened her eyes and looked at him. His face was taut, his jaw clenched.

"That was magnificent." She snuggled toward him and felt the brush of his sex against her thigh. She felt foolish. He hadn't participated. "It also wasn't fair. What about you?"

He kissed her temple. "This was about you."

She shook her head. "I want you to experience what I did." She rolled to her side. "May I?" She gently touched his cock. It was soft and smooth and incredibly hard. "Show me."

He put his hand over hers and curled her fingers around his flesh. Then he guided her to the base. "Up and down," he rasped. "Slowly at first."

At first. She did as he described, gripping him gently as she moved her hand up his shaft. "As you did with me?" At his nod, she continued, setting a modest pace. "Then faster, also as you did with me?" She increased her speed.

He rolled to his back. "Dear God. Yes."

"When do you put this inside me?" Her sex began to pulse again. Was that normal? She wanted to feel that same release he'd given her once more.

He closed his eyes, his face a mask of need. "After we're married."

Her hand stilled, and his eyes opened. He turned his head to focus on her, his pupils dilated.

Married? Had she heard him right? "But we aren't getting married."

He blinked, then flicked a glance down at where she still touched him. "I think we must."

She withdrew her hand and scooted away from him. "Why?"

"I should think it's obvious."

Because of what they'd done. And yes, she supposed that would be the normal course of things. "I don't think it's obvious, actually. I think that's what most would expect, but I am not most people. On the contrary, I've no wish to marry."

Color started to rise in his face, and he twitched twice in quick succession. "Hell." The word shot from him, and the resulting frown gave her to think he hadn't meant to say it.

His "affliction" was surfacing. And it was her fault. "I'm sorry. I don't mean to upset you. It's just...I have enjoyed tonight between us, and I would continue. But I understand if you would rather not."

He turned his head, his neck stretching—another twitch. "My honor will not allow me to."

She'd said she understood—and she did—however, that didn't mean she wasn't disappointed. She slid from the bed. "I'll go."

He sat up. "Bee."

"It's fine." She summoned a smile. "Thank you. For what you gave me. I'll treasure tonight always." Feeling suddenly emotional, she darted from his bedchamber back to the sitting room, where she quickly donned her clothing. The dressing gown in particular was still damp, and she began to shiver as she worked to stuff her feet into her wet slippers.

Quick, before he comes out and sees that you're upset!

Bianca hurried from the sitting room and made her way across the upper floor to her chamber. She moved quickly, praying no one would see her—especially Ash's mother.

At last, she reached her room. Once inside, she went to the fire, which was quite low.

"My lady?" Donnelly's sleepy voice came from the dressing chamber, and a moment later, she appeared, wiping a hand over her eye. "I'm sorry. I dozed off."

"That's fine." Bianca preferred to be alone right then anyway.

"I'll just stir the fire," Donnelly said, already applying herself to the task.

A bigger fire and the warmth it would provide would not come amiss. Bianca was still feeling chilled. And she wasn't sure it was entirely from her clothing.

She walked past Donnelly toward the dressing chamber. "I need to change." A moment later, she was garbed in a fresh night rail. She rushed back to the fireplace and curled herself onto the chair before it.

Donnelly fetched a blanket from the bed and wrapped it about Bianca. Warmth began to soothe her—at least on the outside. Inside, she still felt cold.

"Can I get you anything else?" Donnelly asked.

Bianca tried to smile at her and failed. "No, thank you. Go on back to bed. I went outside to look at the snow, and I just need a few minutes to warm up."

Donnelly nodded. "Of course, my lady." Then she turned and retreated to the dressing room, where her cot was located.

Gradually, heat pervaded Bianca's body, but it wasn't the kind Ash had stoked within her. She tried to identify the reason for the cold, hollow feeling inside her, a feeling that trapped unshed tears at the back of her throat.

She thought of how generous and kind Ash had been all evening and of how she'd stirred his infirmity. The ache inside her intensified. She hated that she'd caused him to be upset.

What a tangle. She considered going back to his room to apologize, but reasoned that would only keep the matter festering between them. Wait, would it agitate and disrupt their friendship? She hadn't considered that. She hadn't considered anything except embracing the delicious moment that had sprung up between them.

And if she went back, could that moment continue? Did she want it to?

Yes.

Groaning, she knocked her head against the cushion of the high-backed chair. She was a wanton, clearly. She wanted Ash, her oldest and dearest friend, but she didn't want to marry him. It wasn't him, it was shackling herself to someone who would control her life. Living with Calder and his dismal behavior was bad enough.

Then there was the fact that Ash was an earl, and he had to be in London part of the year. She would hate being away from her home. On the other hand, Ash had obviously loved it—and it had changed him for the better. Or so he said. Could she grow to appreciate it too?

She opened her eyes, startled, and sat up in the chair. Was she considering his proposal?

She wasn't entirely rejecting it. She couldn't. Not when she thought of the way he'd made her feel. For a while, she'd lost control and for someone who liked to manage everything, it had been a surprisingly heady feeling. Because she knew she could trust Ash.

What's more, if she didn't marry him, she'd never know what happened next. She wasn't sure she could go a lifetime with that sort of frustration.

After staring into the fire for she didn't know how long, Bianca rose from the chair and padded to the bed. Burrowing under the covers, she closed her eyes and tried to make sense of how quickly and drastically her life seemed to have changed. All because she'd found Ash again.

The boy who'd rescued her. And maybe the only one who ever would.

~

*A*sh purposely went down to breakfast later than usual the following morning. Aside from having been up half the night tortured by thoughts of Bianca and the future he now desperately wanted and apparently couldn't have, he didn't particularly want to see her or his mother.

So it was with hope that he entered the breakfast room, only to stop short at seeing both women seated at the table. He took a deep breath and counted to three, but a shudder passed over him nonetheless, twisting his neck and cresting across his shoulders.

They swung their heads toward him, one with a tense, expectant expression, the other smiling. His mother spoke. "Good morning! I was wondering if you'd perhaps taken ill. You didn't go out in the snow last night, did you? I know how much you love a snowfall, especially the first one."

"I did, in fact." His gaze connected with Bianca's, but just for a moment, because he abruptly turned to fetch a plate from the sideboard. A twitch pricked his frame, and he rolled his shoulder.

The footman was at the sideboard, a mild look of confusion marring his brow. Typically, he would serve Ash's plate and deliver it to the table. Today, however, Ash shook his head, and the footman retreated.

After filling his plate, Ash went to sit down. He stared at the food and wondered why he'd taken so much. He wasn't sure he could eat. Not with his fondest desire sitting across from him.

"Alas, the snow has stopped," his mother continued. "But that means Lady Bianca can go to her sister's house today."

"We'll see," Ash said, picking up his knife to spread jam on his toast. He willed his body to behave, but his head tipped to the side. "The snow does not appear to be melting, and if the temperature doesn't warm quickly enough, she won't be able to leave. Not in a carriage, anyway. I suppose she could ride to her sister's."

"Surely it's too cold for such a journey," his mother declared. She turned her head to Bianca. "You may have to stay another night."

"I won't mind," Bianca said.

Hell. One more night under the same roof with her? Last night had been agonizing enough.

Ash couldn't look at her. Instead, he focused on eating his toast, which tasted and crumbled like sand in his mouth.

His mother pushed back her chair. "If you'll excuse me, I'm going to repair to my sitting room to work on plans for the St. Stephen's Day party. There are so many lists to make." She beamed at both of them. "I'm so thrilled to help."

Ash was glad to see her so happy. He knew it had been hard for her to leave their home in Hartwell, but she'd insisted on coming here to support him as he learned how to be an earl. This would give her the chance to spend time in Hartwell and see Shield's End put to good use. "I daresay it will end up benefiting everyone that the duke decided to forgo hosting the party. I can think of no one better to lead the charge." He smiled at her and forced himself to take another bite of toast.

"Not me," his mother said. "Lady Bianca is leading things. I am a happy soldier." She started to rise, and Ash got to his feet. He was having even more trouble chewing and swallowing this bite of toast. He was also having difficulty avoiding Bianca's gaze.

Perhaps he should quit the room too. "Do you need help, Mother?" he asked.

She waved him back down. "No. Finish your breakfast. I'll see you later." With a final cheerful nod toward both of them, she turned and left.

Ash gave up on the toast and moved on to his eggs. They tasted like...nothing. At least he could swallow them down without much effort.

Bianca glanced toward the footman, her eyes furtive. After the fourth time, it was evident she was hoping the footman would leave.

Ash turned toward the retainer. "Would you go and speak with the head groom and ask if he thinks Lady Bianca will be able to travel today?"

"Yes, my lord." The footman spun about and departed.

"Better?" Ash only looked briefly at her before taking another bite of tasteless eggs.

"I'm sorry I can't leave," Bianca blurted.

"We'll see if that's true."

"Please don't be angry with me."

Now he pinned her with a direct stare. "I'm not."

"Well, I am."

He cocked his head—on purpose—and blinked. "You're angry with me?"

Her eyes widened in horror. "No! I'm angry with *me*. I never meant to cause you...distress last night. I feel awful."

"You mustn't. It wasn't your fault."

Her expression turned dubious, her brows briefly arching. "I'm not sure I agree with you, but I won't argue."

"I'm the one who must apologize," he said. "I never should have allowed things to progress."

"It wasn't your fault at all. I'm to blame. I'm the one who took my clothes off and tried to seduce you. Then I touched your—"

"Bee. I'd rather you didn't talk about it." Reliving their torrid encounter was bad enough, but hearing her describe it was a torment he wasn't prepared to endure. A tremor worked through his neck and down his arm.

Quiet reigned once more. Ash surrendered the eggs and moved on to the kippers. After one bite, he decided he was finished. He looked toward her as she gazed out the window, her face in profile. The gentle slope of her nose and the strong jut of her chin were so distinctive. He could identify her at fifty paces from among a field of women. And the rest would pale in comparison.

She abruptly stood, and Ash quickly got to his feet. "I think it's time for our snowball fight."

"I'm not sure that's a good idea."

She laughed gaily. "Come on." She gave him a tart, teasing look, and he was helpless to resist her allure. "I think you will feel better if you can throw a snowball at me. Or ten."

He would feel better if he could marry her. If he could claim to the world that she belonged to him —that he loved her beyond measure.

He loved her?

Of course. That was what the empty ache in his chest signified—the loss of something he'd only just realized he wanted more than anything. A countess was necessary, but Bianca was absolutely vital. He couldn't imagine anyone else sharing his life or his bed.

Suddenly, the idea of throwing snowballs— maybe not at her—sounded exactly perfect.

CHAPTER 8

*D*espite her tall boots, heavy cloak, and extra-thick gloves, Bianca was quite wet. Making and throwing snowballs would do that, she supposed. Still, she wouldn't trade it. Seeing Ash laugh was worth any price. Being the one to provoke that laughter was a gift.

She'd seen the disappointment and sadness in the rigidity of his body the moment he'd walked into the breakfast room. Knowing she was the cause of his upset had nearly torn her in two.

Then, when she'd apologized and tried to take responsibility, he'd been an utter gentleman. He was, she realized, without compare.

She looked askance at where he was building his snowman. They were having a contest to see whose would be taller without falling over—he'd promised not to go higher than her head to keep things fair.

Only he wasn't there.

Too late, she heard the soft squish of snow behind her. Just before the coldness seeped down the back of her cloak.

Gasping, she spun about, her jaw gaping. His

eyes danced as he shrugged. She promptly burst out laughing.

He joined in, and a good minute passed before she could speak. "I deserved that." She'd crept up on him earlier and pressed a small snowball on the back of his neck. He'd nearly jumped out of his skin.

"You absolutely did," he said.

She realized she still held snow in her hand. She'd scooped it up to add to her sculpture. Curling her hand around the cold mass, she started to throw—

Only to have him launch toward her. She tried to back out of his reach, but her foot slipped in the snow, and there was nothing she could do to keep from going down. Her legs slid out from beneath her, and she fell back into the soft snow.

Ash's eyes widened, and then the heavens made things right, and he slipped too.

His arms windmilled, and he fell forward, managing to pivot so that he landed beside her. Unfortunately, he got a face full of snow.

He lifted his head and turned it toward her. Snow clung to his brow, his nose, his chin making him into a living snowman. Bianca dissolved into laughter once again.

He grinned. "Do I look absurd?"

Bianca caught her breath. "You look like my brother if his outside matched his inside." She immediately grimaced. "I probably shouldn't have said that."

"It's not as if I will tell him. Your secret—all your secrets—are safe with me."

She wasn't sure she had any secrets. Except for last night. And he knew about that one. What he didn't know was how deep her regret went or how conflicted she felt, especially in this moment.

She enjoyed being with him. He made her feel cared for and respected. If she was going to wed, he was the type of husband she would want.

Propping herself on her elbow, she turned to her side. She was immediately sorry as the cold wet saturated the clothing covering her hip. There was no help for it now. She was going to need a bath no matter what.

She watched as he wiped the snow from his face. "Is your offer from last night still available?"

His hand froze, then jolted—a tremor, she believed. He finished clearing the snow away and pierced her with the warm chocolate of his eyes. "It will be until you decide to marry someone else."

Her breath tripped in her chest. "I wouldn't. It isn't that I don't want to marry you." On the contrary...she *might*. "It's that I don't want to marry anyone."

"Then we may both die unwed." He said it in a wry way, but it was an incredibly sad thought.

"Well, that's depressing."

He laughed softly as he turned to his side to face her. "It's the truth. Sometimes the truth isn't what we want, but it's what we must live with."

She thought of his infirmity and the pain it had brought him—and how he learned to cope and survive. Admiration crested within her. "You're an extraordinary man. That's why I want you to know it isn't you."

He nodded. "I understand." He lifted his voice to a higher pitch, mimicking her. "*If* I were to wed, I would wed you!" He lowered his tone once more. "Is that the right of it?"

He grinned, and she scooped up another bit of snow and tossed it at his chest. His eyes widened, then narrowed. His jaw clenched just before he launched forward and pushed her to her back once more.

Grabbing her hands, he held them above her head. She gasped again, but it had nothing to do with the cold at her back and everything to do with the way he straddled her.

"Has anyone ever told you that you're diabolical?" he asked.

"My siblings, I'm sure." Heat and joy rushed through her, along with a jolting heat given the way he held her arms and the manner in which their pelvises touched. Why was she declining his marriage proposal? "It's not just that I don't wish to marry. If I *were* to marry you, I'd have to live in London, and I don't want to. I like it here. No, I love it here." Especially *here*. With him.

"We're back to that?" He lifted a shoulder, and she wasn't sure if it was a twitch or not. No, she knew—this one was on purpose. "Only part of the year, or you can stay here year-round. Though I would miss you dreadfully."

She would miss him too. When he left after the new year, she feared her heart would break.

"What if I bought you a house outside London? Then we could see each other regularly and you wouldn't have to live in the city. I'm sure there's a local cause we can find for you to dedicate your time and passion to."

The sun emerged from behind a cloud, its rays already working to melt the snow around them, just as her resolve was suddenly faltering. He was too perfect. Too wonderful. No, he was simply Ash.

"Together, we could choose a house and make it feel like here," he continued. "Like home."

She already knew what home felt like. Ash.

"My goodness, what are you doing?" Mrs. Rutledge's voice rent the air and was followed by a nervous laugh.

Ash nearly jumped off Bianca, springing to his feet and quickly helping her to stand. "Nothing. We slipped."

"That explains it," his mother said with another awkward laugh. "I think you both need a bath right away. Even though the sun is out, you must be freezing."

"Now that I am wet, yes," Bianca admitted.

As they started toward the house, Mrs. Rutledge said, "I came to speak with you about the party. I do think we should ask Thornaby and Keldon for support."

"No," Bianca and Ash said in unison. Their gazes met around Ash's mother, who walked between them.

"Whyever not? They'd be more than happy to help, and Keldon's mother is a friend of mine. She'd be disappointed if I didn't ask."

"We don't need to trouble anyone," Ash said with a flick of his shoulder. "Let us surprise everyone with what we come up with."

Bianca nodded enthusiastically. "Exactly. I'm sure Poppy and Gabriel will help—we can manage it between us."

Mrs. Rutledge frowned slightly as the footman opened the door. "If you say so."

"We do," Ash assured her.

His mother went in first, followed by Bianca, and then Ash.

"They both need warm baths," Mrs. Rutledge said to the butler while he closed the door. The retainer nodded and took himself off.

Bianca moved to Ash's side and whispered, "Too bad we can't take one together."

He gave her the most scalding stare she'd ever

received, and the unfulfilled ache inside her began to grow again. "You're going to ruin me completely." His voice was barely audible next to her ear above the pounding of her blood.

Today, Bianca had had a glimpse of what their life together could be like. The prospect was beyond tempting.

~

*I*f there had ever been a more perfect day, Ash wasn't aware of it. Not in his life. Not in anyone's life. He'd dare anyone to best the sheer joy and delight of spending time with Bianca. And that was *after* she'd declined his marriage proposal.

Oh, it still stung, but he possessed something tonight he hadn't the night before: hope. She'd been flirtatious and provocative as well as apologetic and possibly plagued by regret. He didn't wish her to feel bad, truly, but if that remorse moved her to change her mind, he would consider himself fortunate indeed.

Reality—and cynicism—crowded his buoyant thoughts. If he hoped to persuade her to alter course, he was nearly out of time. Tomorrow, she would be on her way to her sister's. The snow had melted considerably that afternoon, but not quickly enough for her to arrive at Darlington Abbey before the sun went down. She would, however, be able to leave in the morning.

He had a choice—he could lie here in bed and wait for something to happen, or he could get up and pursue the future he wanted. Put like that, there was no choice at all.

Ash threw the covers off and reached for his banyan, drawing it closed over his nightshirt. Before he could think better of his intentions, he went from the bedchamber into the sitting room. In a trice, he opened the door.

And immediately stopped cold.

Standing there in her dressing gown was Bianca, her dark hair hanging in a thick plait over her right shoulder. Her brilliant blue eyes regarded him with surprise. "I didn't even knock," she said.

"I was coming to see you."

"Were you?" She sounded slightly breathless.

He clasped her elbow and drew her inside, quickly closing the door behind her. "Bee—"

She put her finger against his lips. "Shh. I came to see you. I get to speak."

With her touching his mouth, he wasn't sure he would hear a word she said. His cock was already at full attention, his body thrumming with keen desire.

He answered by nodding.

"Good." She lowered her hand, and he resisted the urge to snag her fingertip between his teeth. "I've changed my mind. I will marry you."

Joy burst in his chest, and he just barely caught himself from yelling an expletive. At the worst of his affliction, that had been a rather common occurrence when he was excited. And since this was potentially the most spectacular moment of his life, it made sense he would react in the same manner. He was just glad he'd stopped himself before he drove her away for good.

The reality of what she said settled into him. "Do you mean it?" he whispered. Fear edged out his happiness. What would she do when he inevitably didn't control himself? When something leapt from his mouth, or he suffered a fit of twitching that would draw all manner of attention?

"I do."

"I think I might have changed *my* mind."

Deep lines furrowed her brow as she stepped closer to him until they almost touched. "Why?" She shook her head. "No, never mind. You can't."

"Yes, I can. You shouldn't marry me. I'm...broken." He turned away from her.

But he didn't get very far. She rushed around him, blocking his path. "You are not." She put her hands on her hips and glared at him. "Don't ever say that. You are perfect."

He laughed. The reaction was partly beyond his control, but it was also fitting. "I am anything but that. I don't want to subject you to this —to me."

She raked him with her gaze from the top of his red hair to the tips of his bare feet. "Too late. You already subjected me to you, and I'm rather fond of you."

His chest constricted as his heart swelled. "You've seen... It can get much worse. Sometimes things come out of my mouth, things I can't control."

Her lids drooped over her eyes. "Is that all?"

"The twitching can be...violent. I've been known to frighten people, though not as much now."

She touched his face, her soft hand caressing his stubbled jaw. "How have you borne it? When I think of what you must have endured at school and in London, I am filled with outrage."

"London was not so terrible, but as you know, school was horrendous. If I hadn't scored such high marks and earned the care of the head of my college, I am confident they would have sent me home."

"You have survived." She stroked his cheek. "As I said before, you are an extraordinary man. I would be proud to call you my husband, if you'll let me."

His fear began to ease, but he was still confounded by her reversal. "Why did you change your mind?"

She cupped his face in her hands and stared earnestly into his eyes. "*I* didn't change it—you did. You showed me what I would be missing, what I would regret. When you said today that you wouldn't marry until I did, I knew that I couldn't consign you to a life of being alone."

He barked out a laugh. "So you took pity on me?"

She grimaced, letting her hands slide down his neck to his collarbones. "That didn't come out right. I don't want you to be alone. More than that, I don't want you to be with anyone but me."

He wrapped his arms around her and pulled her against his chest. "Good, because I don't want anyone other than you. You're certain you can live with my disease?"

"Since I don't think I can live without you, I would say, definitively, *yes.*"

"Bee." He lowered his head and brushed his lips against hers. Before he could say he loved her, she kissed him in wild abandon, her mouth opening beneath his.

Her tongue touching his was the spark that set his entire world aflame. Lifting her, he carried her into his bedroom and laid her gently on the bed.

"This seems familiar," she murmured.

"This night is not going to end the same," he pledged.

She reached for him as he shrugged out of his banyan. "Good."

In a flurry of limbs, they disrobed. Ash paused to take in the sheer beauty of her body. He bent his head to worship at her breast, taking her nipple into his mouth and suckling until she threaded her fingers through his hair and cried out his name.

He slid his hand down her belly until he found the curls cloaking her sex. She was hot and wet for him already. The moment he touched her clitoris, she shuddered.

"Please. Ash."

He stroked her, increasing speed as she moved her hips in concert with his touch.

"Fill me. Now." The plea was dark and desperate. She grasped at his shoulders as she rose off the bed to meet his caresses.

He slipped his finger into her sheath, filling her as she asked. She whimpered, and he felt her muscles clench around him. He pressed on her clitoris, and she flew apart, her legs shaking as her cries grew higher. He covered her mouth with his, taking her passion into himself.

He didn't wait for her to return from beyond. Sitting back, he positioned himself at her sex.

Her eyes opened, and the blue of her irises was so clear, so vivid in her wonder, that he paused. He leaned forward and kissed her softly, then eased slowly into her sheath. She sucked in a breath and held it. Her eyes slitted but didn't close as he continued on. When he was buried completely inside her, he paused, waiting for her to adjust.

"Do you feel all right?" he asked. He hadn't ever done this with a virgin, and he didn't want to cause her undue pain.

She finally exhaled. "I think so. It feels strange."

"My apologies. From what I understand, the next time will be much better for you."

"Lucky for me, I will have many, many next times with you."

Love swelled within him. Then she moved, a slight hitch of her hips.

Her eyes widened briefly. "I didn't mean to do that! I think I twitched." She giggled.

"You mean my disease is catching?" he asked in mock horror.

"Perhaps, and I don't care. It's who you are, and I wouldn't change a thing about you. Maybe one thing, actually. I think I might like you to move."

"With pleasure." He withdrew and thrust gently forward, again and again until her breath began to shorten and her eyes closed in what looked like ecstasy. He clasped her thigh and guided it to his waist. "Wrap your legs around me, love."

She did just that, opening herself to him so that he sank even deeper into her. She moaned softly. "I think this time is quite nice." Her legs tightened around him, and he lost conscious thought.

They moved together in an ever-quickening pace, their bodies finding a magical rhythm. He felt the blood rush to his cock and knew he was close. Reaching between them, he stroked her clitoris again, determined to coax another orgasm from her or at least try his damnedest.

Just before he came, her muscles clamped down around him. He cried out her name and thrust deep, spilling himself into her. Pleasure spiraled through him, tossing him into unparalleled bliss.

Some moments later, when he was fully back within himself, he shifted his weight from her. He kissed her cheek, her jaw, her mouth.

She sighed into him as he left her body. He tried to move away, but she held him close. "I'll be right back," he whispered. "We should clean up."

Her eyes opened, and he saw what he felt: bone-deep satisfaction. And, maybe, love.

"I don't want to go," she said softly.

"Then don't. We are betrothed."

Her lips curled into a smile. "As good as wed. Will I really be the Countess of Buckleigh?"

He nodded, still thinking how strange that sounded.

"I would have been just as happy as Mrs. Rutledge." She yawned.

Her proclamation warmed him as he left the bed to get a cloth. When he returned, she took the cloth and tidied herself then he tucked her beneath the coverlet. By the time he returned to snuggle beside her, she was already asleep.

Smiling to himself, he pressed his lips to her temple and whispered, "I love you."

CHAPTER 9

Though it was melting, snow still dotted the landscape as they traveled to Hartwood. Bianca nestled closer to Ash in his coach, not only for the warmth he offered but because she found she simply liked to be next to him. Her maid and his valet rode behind them in Calder's coach. Ash had decided to bring his valet in case Calder invited him to stay. Bianca would do everything she could to make that happen.

Now that she decided she couldn't live without Ash, she wanted their life together to start immediately. "Do we need to have the banns read?"

They'd discussed the timing of the wedding that morning at breakfast. His mother had been overjoyed at the news of their betrothal. She'd also said she wasn't surprised given their behavior yesterday. Then she'd said the sweetest thing: "It will be so lovely to have a daughter again."

Fighting back tears, Bianca hadn't known what to say. She'd never had a mother before.

"Would you rather I buy a license and we marry tomorrow?" Ash asked.

"Could we?"

He laughed. "Not tomorrow, but how about this Thursday?"

"Hmm." She tapped her finger against her chin, pretending to consider. Dropping her hand to her lap, she grinned at him. "As luck would have it, I am free."

"Brilliant." He kissed her as he'd done a dozen or more times on the journey so far. Too bad they were pulling up the drive to Hartwood, or she might have tried to coax him into more than kissing...

The coach rumbled to a stop, and Bianca exhaled in resignation. "I'll apologize now for my brother's behavior." She was a trifle nervous he would say something about Ash's fighting, but resolved that it didn't matter.

When they were out of the coach, she took Ash's arm and gave him an encouraging smile that was as much for him as it was for her. They walked toward the house, and Truro, the butler, opened the door to greet them.

"Welcome home, Lady Bianca," he said.

"Thank you, Truro. This is the Earl of Buckleigh, my betrothed." Saying that out loud sparked a rush of joy and excitement. She wanted to shout it from the turret in the northwest corner so all of Hartwood and Hartwell could hear.

Truro was quite possibly the most unflappable butler in the history of butlers. He didn't register even an inkling of surprise nor did he demonstrate any other emotion. He inclined his head and said, "May I offer my deepest congratulations?"

She beamed at him and at last saw the barest hint of a smile. "Thank you. Will you ask my brother to meet us in the drawing room?"

"Certainly." He took her cloak and other accessories while a footman took Ash's things.

Bianca relooped her hand through Ash's arm and led him through the entrance hall into the inner hall and then right into the drawing room. "My brother is going to be ecstatic to be rid of me."

"You think so?" Ash asked.

"I know so. He keeps grumbling about me having a Season, and now neither of us has to bother with it."

They stood in the middle of the drawing room, and Ash turned to her. "Will you be coming to London with me?" They hadn't gotten to discussing that in the coach.

Bianca hated the prospect of leaving her home, but she hated the prospect of not being with him even more. "Yes. Anywhere we're together is my home now."

Smiling, he leaned down to kiss her again, but Calder's arrival interrupted them.

"What the devil is going on?" His angry voice carried through the drawing room. It was the most emotion she'd heard from him since he'd come back to Hartwood. "Truro referred to Buckleigh as your betrothed." He glowered at Ash.

"You really need to work on polite greetings," Bianca said with impatience. "It's nice to see you, Calder. Allow me to present my *betrothed*, the Earl of Buckleigh."

"I bloody well know him," Calder growled. "And he is not your betrothed. I haven't given you permission to wed. But that is beside the point right now. How is it that you went to Poppy's and returned home with him?"

Bianca felt Ash stiffen and then a tremor shuddered through him. "I didn't go to Poppy's. I was trapped by—"

His eyes snapped with fury. "You didn't go to Darlington Abbey? You lied to me?"

"I took a detour. I wanted to speak with Ash about where to have the St. Stephen's Day party." She sniffed and notched up her chin. "Which we have resolved, thank you very much. Or not, actually, since you're the reason we had to come up with an alternate location."

"I don't give a damn about the bloody party." He clenched his jaw as he continued to glare at Ash. "And there will be no wedding."

"There *will*." She clutched Ash's arm and tried to imbue him with her support and love. *Love? Oh yes.*

Ash twitched several times in quick succession, as well as coughed and cleared his throat.

Calder's lip curled. "There will *not*. I won't allow you to marry Buckleigh. He's too volatile. Just look at him. It's as if he can't control himself."

"Shut up!" Ash pulled away from Bianca, and for a brief moment, she worried he might go after Calder. Which Calder wholly deserved. "I have a disease, and sometimes—particularly when I'm provoked—it's beyond my control." His chest rose and fell rapidly as he fought to regain command of himself.

Bianca touched Ash's arm but looked to her brother. "I'll marry whom I choose. I'm of age."

Calder's eyes narrowed with distrust as he regarded Ash. Then he turned his attention to Bianca. "While that is true, your settlement is under my control until you are twenty-five. If I don't approve of your husband, you don't receive the money."

Her jaw dropped as outrage curled through her. "You would keep what Papa intended me to have?" Why had her father even set things up in that fashion? Because he'd trusted Calder not to be a cold-hearted monster.

"He gave me the management of it—and you—

for a reason. I would be remiss if I didn't do my duty."

Bianca threw her hands up. "You and your duty. Forget family or loyalty or *love*." She glared at him and fully surrendered to her anger and disappointment toward him. "I don't know who you are, but you aren't my brother. I don't need your approval, and I don't want it either. Keep my settlement. It seems money is all that concerns you anymore. I hope it will make you happy."

Calder frowned deeply. "You're making a mistake marrying him."

"I'm not the one who will regret this day, Calder. I'm going to stay with Poppy until the wedding on Thursday. If you can't at least be polite to the man I love, I ask that you stay away—from the wedding, from us, and from St. Stephen's Day."

He exhaled with exasperation. "I've told you I've no interest in—"

She held up her hand. "Don't bother. We're leaving now. You can finally be alone, which I think is what you want." Bianca took Ash's hand and pulled him from the drawing room through the inner hall to the main stairs.

"I need to tell Donnelly to pack my things as quickly as possible," she said, starting up the stairs.

"Did I hear you right?" he asked, tugging on her hand as they reached the landing.

She turned to him, her mind whirring through her ire and frustration. "What?"

"Did I hear you say that I'm the man you love?"

All the negative emotions crowding within her faded away. She glanced down at the floor, suddenly feeling rather shy. "Yes."

He touched her chin, lifting it. "Of all the times for you to become timid." He laughed, then cupped her cheek. "I love you, Bianca, and I'm overjoyed you love me in return."

"Of course I do. I'm just so sorry my brother ruined our happiness." She straightened her shoulders. "No, he *tried* to ruin it. And he failed."

"He did manage to take your settlement from you, however." The muscles in Ash's neck flexed, and his head cocked to the side as he coughed. "I'm sorry it came to that."

"I'm not. It doesn't matter, so long as we're together."

Ash pulled her against his chest. "I am the luckiest man in the world."

She twined her arms around his neck. "Then I am the luckiest woman." She stood on her toes and kissed him, but kept the contact brief. She wanted to leave Calder's toxic orbit as soon as possible.

Tugging him up the stairs, she said, "Come, let's hurry. I want to visit Shield's End before we go to Darlington Abbey." She paused just before she reached the first floor and looked up at him. "On second thought, maybe I should just go back to Buck Manor." She narrowed her eyes suggestively.

He let out a soft growl. "You are incredibly wicked, my lady."

"I'm not your lady yet," she teased.

He pulled her to the top step and into his arms once more. "Oh yes, you are. You're mine. For all time."

❧

As Ash helped Bianca into his coach, he cast a final disappointed look at Hartwood's imposing manor house. He wondered if they would ever return. The rest of Bianca's things would be sent to Buck Manor, so there was really no need for her to come back. Not until her brother apologized.

If he apologized. Right now, Ash couldn't see that happening.

They settled into the coach and started toward town where they would stop at Shield's End to speak with the caretaker about the St. Stephen's Day party. Tucket had taken care of the property since long before Ash had been born, and though he was now nearly deaf and not nearly as spry as he'd once been, they wouldn't replace him. His son was a cabinetmaker in the village, and he checked in regularly.

"We should also stop and speak with Alfie Tucket in town," Ash said, thinking he should be made aware of the party along with his father.

"Oh yes, we must." Bianca shook her head. "I'm afraid I'm not thinking quite clearly."

Ash took her hand and gave her a comforting squeeze. "That's to be expected. Let me do the thinking today."

Her answering smile glowed bright with gratitude. "Thank you. I'm still so sorry about Calder."

"You've nothing to apologize for. He'll come around—or he won't. Either way, we will live our lives." Ash cleared his throat as a ripple ran down his neck.

Ever determined, Bianca pressed her lips together. "Yes, we will." She turned her head to look out the window and almost immediately gasped.

Ash bent his head to try to glimpse whatever she saw. "What's wrong?"

"There's smoke."

Leaning forward, Ash craned his neck and caught sight of a plume of smoke rising into the gray sky. He frowned as he conjured a map of the town in his mind. Unease slithered through him

as a shudder twitched his shoulders. It couldn't
be...

Bianca turned her head toward him, her eyes
wide. "That isn't Shield's End, is it?"

Ash's stomach dropped straight through the
bottom of the coach as a wave of fear assaulted
him. "I'm afraid it might be."

For the next several minutes, his anxiety grew.
Bianca clutched his hand ever tighter as it became
evident that the smoke was definitely coming from
Shield's End.

The coach stopped at the end of the lane, and
Ash didn't wait for the footman to open the door.
He bounded out and gaped in anguish at the smoke
billowing from his childhood home.

"Ash!"

He turned to help Bianca down. Her face mir-
rored his pain. "Go," she urged, pushing him toward the house. "I'll send the coach to get help."

"Stay back," he said before letting her go and
dashing down the lane toward the house.

The fire hadn't consumed the structure, but Ash
could see flames licking from the side of the
ground floor. He hoped Tucket wasn't inside. He
lived in a small cottage next to the stable. Ash
raced there in the hope of finding him. When he
wasn't there, ice-cold fear lodged in the center of
Ash's chest.

Running toward the back of the house, Ash
stopped as he caught sight of a pair of men
standing in the yard, staring at the burning structure. When he neared, he saw exactly who they
were, and his fear blackened into rage.

"Moreley! Keldon! What the devil are you doing
here?" he thundered, his hands curling into fists.

They turned in surprise. "Ruddy!" Moreley said,
wiping a hand over his mouth. "Ah—"

"There's been an accident," Keldon said quickly. "Thornaby's inside."

"Where is my caretaker?"

Both men blanched, and Keldon responded, "There's a caretaker?"

Ash swore vehemently as a series of tremors and twitches sailed through his body. "Bianca has taken my coach to get help. Make yourselves useful and fetch water from the well at least, for pity's sake."

Taking off past them, Ash raced into the house and was instantly overcome with a wall of smoke. He coughed and put his hand over his mouth. Untying his cravat, he pulled it from his neck and fashioned a mask, which he tied over his mouth and nose.

Blinking, he tried to assess the situation— where the fire was located and where it was going. At the same time, he called out for the caretaker. "Tucket!" He did this repeatedly as he moved farther into the house. Desperation curdled in Ash's chest.

How was Tucket ever going to hear him?

Satisfied that he'd searched everywhere he could downstairs away from the flames, he went to the stairs. If he went up, he could become trapped. But if he didn't go up and Tucket was up there... Not to mention Thornaby. Much as Ash despised the man, he wouldn't let him die.

Ash started up the stairs and nearly stumbled as he heard the bleat of a goat. A *goat*?

Yes, a goat, being pulled along by Tucket. Ash dashed up to the top. "Thank God, Tucket," he yelled, hoping the man could hear him. "You go down. I'll get the goat!"

Tucket scowled and pulled on the animal's lead. "He's being stubborn."

Ash picked the goat up and was rewarded with several loud bleats. "Go!" he called to Tucket.

The caretaker grasped the railing and started down. Ash walked down the other side of the staircase and reached the bottom first. He waited to make sure Tucket made it to the ground floor. The goat, however, did not appreciate their proximity to the fire as flames were licking the room adjacent to the hall. The animal tried desperately to jump free and to destroy Ash's hearing as well.

Ash clutched the goat more firmly and hurried from the house straight to the yard. He quickly deposited the animal onto the grass, then removed his mask to take several lungfuls of air. Tucket emerged from the house, staggering, and Ash rushed forward to help him.

"Sit down," Ash urged, guiding him away from the structure. "Catch your breath." He spoke loudly and clearly and was glad when Tucket nodded in response.

Ash looked back at the house as he settled the caretaker onto the grass. Why was Thornaby still inside?

"There's another goat upstairs," Tucket said between deep breaths. "And a fancy gent. He was trying to get the goat down, but she was even more stubborn than this one." Tucket threw a disgruntled scowl at the goat who was now grazing.

Another goat? Why the hell were there goats in his house? Ash swore loudly—he couldn't help himself—and went back to the house. And where the hell were Keldon and Moreley with the water?

Ash's second trip inside was much worse than the first. He affixed the mask over his face, but the smoke was thick and acrid. He ran to the stairs and registered that the fire was edging closer. The other staircase was on the side with the raging fire,

so this was their only way out aside from jumping
out a window.

Spurred by desperation, Ash darted up the
stairs. "Thornaby!" Ash called his name several
times and was answered by the distant bleating of a
goat. Following the sound, Ash found them in the
bedchamber that had belonged to his parents.
Smoke filled the room. Thornaby stood near the
bed, bent over and coughing.

Ash grabbed the goat and went to Thornaby.
"Let's go. I have the animal."

Thornaby lifted his head. His eyes were
rimmed with red. He tried to speak between
coughs, but Ash had no idea what he was trying
to say.

"Just go!" Ash ordered, pulling on the man's
bicep.

Thornaby stumbled but began walking toward
the door. Ash picked up the goat and hefted her
over his shoulder. She protested, kicking her legs
and making a horrendous racket.

Ash went as fast as he could. Between the
smoke and the weight, he was beginning to flag. At
the top of the stairs, he looked back and saw that
Thornaby was following, but very slowly.

"Come on, Thornaby! You have to move faster.
The fire is spreading!"

Ash dashed quickly down to the ground floor,
where the goat renewed her fight, landing a nasty
kick against Ash's back. His body jolted, and he
nearly dropped the idiot animal.

Threading his way outside, Ash set the goat
down as hastily as possible. The animal dashed to
join her friend who didn't even look up from his
grassy meal.

Keldon and Moreley had returned. They stood
there with two buckets of water.

"What are you doing?" Ash demanded. "Throw it on the bloody fire!"

"Where's Thornaby?" Moreley asked, his face a ghostly pallor.

Ash swung around and didn't see the viscount. "Bloody fucking hell." Letting out a string of invectives, he stalked back to the house and went inside before he could think better of it.

The smoke was impossible to see through now. Ash bent over to where the visibility was slightly better and looked for Thornaby while calling his name.

The fire was now in the hall, and there, lying at the base of the stairs, was an unconscious Thornaby. Ash swore again, then bent to pick the man up. Grunting, Ash lifted him over his shoulder as he'd done with the goat. God, he hoped he could make it outside. His head was beginning to swim, and he felt as though he couldn't draw breath.

Staggering, he slowly made his way outside. Heat and smoke enveloped him, and the moment he emerged, he dropped to his knees. Thornaby tumbled from his shoulder.

Ash was vaguely aware of voices and of being dragged over the grass. Someone pulled the mask from his face, and sweet air poured into his lungs. A beautiful face floated above him with a halo surrounding her dark hair.

"Am I dead?" Had that come from his mouth?

That was the last thing he recalled before darkness descended.

CHAPTER 10

"*A*sh, wake up, please," Bianca tried not to panic completely. He was breathing, even if his face was the color of his name.

She was aware of the others gathering around them, just as she vaguely registered the group of villagers that had rushed to help. They worked to try to extinguish the fire, but Bianca paid no attention.

Her entire world was suddenly centered on the man lying in the grass, his eyes closed, his dark red lashes still against his face. Though he wouldn't want to, she whispered, "Twitch, jerk, do *something*. Anything." Her voice broke.

At last, his forehead wrinkled. His eyelids fluttered. Then he stared up at her, his beloved brown eyes softening. "Bee." The word was a soft croak, but it was the sweetest sound she'd ever heard.

"Oh, Ash." Tears tracked down her cheeks as she bent over and kissed him—his brow, his cheek, his mouth. Joy rushed through her and washed away the fear.

After a long moment, she sat back. Someone handed her a damp cloth, which she used to wipe the grime away from Ash's face.

"Why were there goats in my house?" he asked. He moved his gaze from her and squinted up at the people surrounding them.

"I'd like to know what Thornaby and his friends are doing here," Bianca said, turning her head to stare at Moreley and Keldon, who stood near Ash's feet.

"We should go see about him," Moreley said, his face turning the color of a persimmon. He spun about and marched off. Keldon hesitated but eventually followed him.

"Where's Thornaby?" Ash asked.

Bianca pointed a few feet away. "Just there. It appears he's still unconscious."

Ash blinked up at her. "Tucket?"

"He's here," Bianca said, touching Tucket's leg.

The caretaker had stood beside her and now knelt down. "My lord, you're the hero of the day."

Ash didn't react to what he said, instead asking, "What happened?"

"I'm not sure how the fire started," Tucket said. "I smelled smoke and saw that the house was burning. When I went closer to investigate, one of those gentlemen," he jabbed his thumb toward Thornaby, Moreley, and Keldon, "ran from the house as if he was on fire." Tucket scoffed. "He wasn't."

"Tell me about the goats," Ash rasped.

"The gent that ran out—the bald one, I know that because his hat fell off—said there were goats in the house and that they started the fire. He said his friends were inside trying to coax them out." Tucket snorted and wiped his hand under his nose. "They sounded like idiots, so I ran in to rescue the animals myself. But damn me if those aren't the most stubborn goats." He threw the pair of animals a glare before adding with regret, "And I'm not as young as I used to be."

"You did what you could," Ash said. "How did these goats start the fire?"

"One of them knocked over a lantern."

Bianca looked toward the trio of bullies and saw that Thornaby was now sitting up.

"We didn't notice until the room was already ablaze—we were busy with the other goat." Thornaby grimaced.

Ash struggled to sit up, and Bianca helped him. "Why the hell were there goats in my house?" he repeated.

Thornaby started to answer. "It was—"

Keldon cut him off. "Thorn!"

Shooting an angry look at Keldon, Thornaby continued. "It was a prank. Like the one we pulled at Oxford."

Bianca felt Ash tense and the pair of tremors that shook his body and made him cock his head to and fro. She put her arm around his shoulders and tried to support him.

"When you let a goat into my room," Ash said flatly, "it made a mess."

Thornaby's face was red, but he didn't falter as he spoke loudly and clearly. "That was our intent. We heard you were going to host the St. Stephen's party here."

"Why would you want to ruin that?" Bianca asked as anger flooded her.

"It wasn't so much to ruin it as to cause trouble for Rud—Buckleigh," Thornaby said, his head dipping in what Bianca hoped was shame.

Ash cleared his throat. "How did you hear about the party?"

"Your mother sent me a note asking if I would help."

Bianca and Ash exchanged a look. Why had she

sent a letter after they'd said no? Was there a chance she'd sent it before asking them?

"She shouldn't have," Ash said coldly. "We don't want your help."

"I don't blame you." Thornaby sounded as if he felt remorse. "I wouldn't want my help either. We never meant to cause a fire."

"It's not our fault!" Moreley cried.

Thornaby glared at him. "It is—we brought the bloody goats. Haven't you acted cowardly enough today? Own up to what we've done." Thornaby looked to Keldon next. "You too. I can't believe you both abandoned me." He gestured toward Tucket. "That old man has more courage than both of you put together."

"You owe Ash an apology," Bianca demanded.

"They owe him restitution," Tucket said. "The house will have to be rebuilt."

It was true. Though the villagers were working on passing water from the well to the house, they couldn't keep up with the flames.

Thornaby struggled to stand, but Keldon and Moreley helped him. He weaved his way over to Ash, who also got up with Bianca's and Tucket's assistance.

"Words cannot convey how sorry I am about your house," Thornaby said. "How sorry all of us are." He indicated the men flanking him.

"I want to hear them say it," Bianca pressed. "And you'll apologize for everything. The shooting competition and everything you ever did or even thought about doing at Oxford. You all make me sick."

None of them could look at her. To a man, they dropped their gazes to the ground.

After a moment, Thornaby lifted his toward

Ash. "We've treated you awfully—from Oxford until today. But no more. I owe you my life."

"Yes, you do," Bianca spat, thinking he didn't deserve to be rescued by Ash.

Ash touched her arm, and she looked up at him to see that he did not appear as furious as she was, at least not anymore.

"I'm sorry too," Keldon said. "Truly. We just meant to cause trouble, nothing serious. When you left the house party the other day, several of the guests were upset. They believed we'd somehow driven you to go."

"You did." Bianca growled low in her throat.

Thornaby nodded. "I was angry that people were siding with Buckleigh."

"There are no sides," Ash said quietly. "That's all in your imagination."

"Yes." Thornaby sounded utterly defeated, and Bianca wanted to dance with glee.

"Moreley?" Bianca prompted. "I believe it's your turn."

"I, ah, I'm sorry. For everything. We won't bother you again."

"Except for rebuilding his house and supporting his St. Stephen's Day party," Thornaby said, his eyes gleaming with determination.

Bianca fixed each of them with a stony glower. "Only we have no place to hold it now."

"You can use Thornhill," Thornaby readily suggested.

"I'd rather not," Bianca said coolly.

Ash shook his head and coughed. "It's too far. I would host it at Buck Manor, but that's also too far."

"It's a pity your brother won't host it," Keldon said.

Yes, it was. Bianca's anger at him sprouted anew. "That is not an option."

"Is Thornhill really too far?" Thornaby asked. "It's only five miles. We can transport people, and whoever needs to stay overnight can do so. We'll make it work. Just tell me what we need to do."

"You'll let my wife and my mother manage everything, and I mean *everything*. You will take their orders, and you won't complain or rebel."

Thornaby nodded, then blinked, cocking his head to the side. "Your wife?"

Ash put his arm around Bianca's waist, and she pressed into his side, reveling in his warmth and basking in the joy of being alive—with him. "Bianca. We will be wed next week. Forgive us for not inviting you to the breakfast." He said the last with more than a hint of sarcasm.

"I wish you both a hearty—and heartfelt—congratulations." Thornaby tried to smile but gave up. "I wouldn't expect to be invited."

"It's settled, then." Ash exhaled, and his shoulder twitched against Bianca.

"Come, let's get you to the coach. I want to take you home so you can rest."

"I won't leave the house. Not until the fire's out." He looked at the burning structure, and she felt his body go rigid. "My mother is going to be devastated."

Bianca flicked a glance toward the trio of miscreants. They hung their heads in shame.

Ash kissed her temple. "I'm fine now, my love. Let me help with the effort to put out the flames."

"I'll help too," she said.

"So will we." Keldon started toward the line passing water. Moreley and Thornaby joined him.

Bianca encircled Ash's waist and squeezed him

tight. "I'm just glad you're safe. When I think of what could have happened…"

"Shh, my love." He brushed his lips against her cheek. "I am here with you, where I plan to stay for a very, very long time."

She looked up at him with love and admiration. "Forever, I hope."

His lips curled into a happy smile. "Forever."

CHAPTER 11

The day of Bianca and Ash's wedding dawned cold and gray. Ash would have loved snow, but he also wanted to be able to get from Buck Manor to the Hartwell Church and back to Buck Manor for the wedding breakfast without incident.

And so it was with great delight that he and Bianca emerged from the coach at Buck Manor only to have a dusting of snowflakes settle upon them.

Laughing, Bianca looked up to the sky. "What a perfect gift for our wedding day."

Ash smiled down at her. "I arranged it special."

She slid him a glance of sheer disbelief, then laughed again. "I shouldn't put it past you, actually. You have been an absolute hero for everyone, so why not for me?"

He curled his arms around her waist and brought her against him so he could kiss her. The contact was brief, but incredibly heady. "I only care about being a hero for you."

"They're here!" the Marchioness of Darlington called from the doorway. She'd left the church with her husband and Ash's mother as soon as the ceremony had finished so they could be here to oversee the wedding breakfast preparations.

Ash and Bianca had visited with the vicar for a while, primarily to discuss plans for rebuilding his house. The entire village was eager to see his property made whole again.

And no one was more eager than Thornaby.

Ash guided his wife into his house—no, *their* house—where a line of guests was waiting in the hall, Thornaby among them. Moreley and Keldon were also there. Bianca hadn't wanted to include any of them, but Ash had persuaded her that it was time to truly put the past behind him. He only hoped they were as committed to that as they professed to be.

He and Bianca spent the next half hour greeting people, followed by a joyous wedding breakfast in the dining room. Afterward, they withdrew to the drawing room, where they drank champagne. Ash watched with pride and love as his countess laughed and spoke with everyone in attendance. Perhaps she didn't laugh with Thornaby and the others, but she was polite and they were effusive in their kindness and praise.

"You're a lucky man, Buckleigh." Thornaby came up behind him, prompting Ash to turn.

"Thank you. I am." While Ash appreciated the man's reversal, he was also incredibly puzzled by it. "I hope you'll forgive me for asking, but after so many years of you torturing me, I find myself wondering what led you to make such a change in your behavior."

"I would forgive you anything," Thornaby said earnestly. "And I mean that. You saved my life. There is something rather clarifying about nearly dying. My life came into a focus I'd never seen before." He glanced at the floor, then sipped his champagne. When he looked at Ash again, there was a weight in his gaze Ash had never seen before.

"I've always felt inadequate," Thornaby admitted. "You didn't know this, but I struggled at Oxford. Reading was very difficult for me. Words and letters—and numbers, even—would jumble in my vision."

"I didn't know that. You always behaved as if you knew and excelled at everything." Ash didn't mask the wryness in his tone.

A small smile flitted across Thornaby's mouth. "It's terrible to say, but I understood your...challenges."

As if provoked by Thornaby's mention of his disease, a shudder rippled across Ash's shoulders, and he tipped his head to the side. "Why is that terrible?"

"Because I was horrible to you because of them." Thornaby grimaced. "It made me feel better about my weaknesses to exploit yours. If that isn't abhorrent, I don't know what is. That you could forgive me for how I treated you, especially for causing your house to burn—"

Ash saw the tears in Thornaby's eyes despite the man quickly blinking them away. "I do forgive you. Because what good would it do to continue to hold a grudge? That certainly doesn't benefit me. As you said, I'm a lucky man, and I intend to be grateful."

"What a beautiful sentiment," Thornaby said in soft wonder.

Ash considered Thornaby's revelation. "I do understand your coping behavior. I chose a different path—I used to hit people."

Thornaby's eyes widened. "You never hit me."

"I was too small." Ash chuckled. "You—or more likely Moreley—would have pounded me into the dirt. Actually, Moreley did do that once."

"So he told me." Thornaby dipped his chin in apology. "I think I missed that. Whom did you hit?"

"Many people. Men, I should clarify. I was a pugilist in London."

Thornaby gasped in surprise. "Were you? How extraordinary. And that helped your affliction?"

Ash nodded. "Boxing gave me strength, obviously, but also courage to face others as well as myself and my limitations. It also showed me that I wasn't as limited as I'd thought." He grinned. "I was quite good at hitting people."

"I think I'd like to see that." Thornaby cocked his head to the side. "Could you teach me?"

"I don't see why not." Ash marveled at how far they'd come in such a short time.

"Thank you." Thornaby lightly clasped his bicep. "I'm grateful for your forgiveness and, dare I say, friendship."

Ash waggled his brows at him. "Go ahead and dare. Now, if you'll excuse me, I need to go and speak with my brother-in-law."

Thornaby inclined his head with a smile and let go of Ash's arm. Ash lifted his glass in a silent toast, then strode toward the Marquess of Darlington, who stood near the windows, his focus trained on the champagne in his hand.

"Darlington," Ash said. "You look as though you're in need of cheer."

The marquess shook his head and blinked. "'Tis nearly the season for that, I suppose. Sorry, I was ruminating."

"May I ask about what?"

"Mostly about Hartwell House and how badly

it's in need of repair." Darlington grimaced. "Never mind. After the fire, you are up to your eyeballs in repairs."

"Reconstruction, you mean," Ash said wryly. "Bianca and I are looking forward to St. Nicholas Day tomorrow at Hartwell House."

"Yes, it should be quite...cheerful."

Ash laughed softly. "Indeed. As you said, it is the season for it. Come, let us join our wives." A thrill danced up Ash's spine. He loved referring to Bianca as his wife.

When they arrived, the third woman had left so that it was just Bianca and her sister. They were animatedly discussing their brother.

"I still can't believe he refused to give you your settlement," the marchioness said crossly. "I plan to speak with him as soon as possible. It's bad enough he didn't come today."

"To be fair, I didn't invite him," Bianca said.

"I did." Ash had reasoned that as long as he'd changed his mind and decided to include the men who'd bullied him and burned his house to the ground, he ought to also invite Bianca's brother, even if he'd behaved in an utterly wretched manner.

"You did?" A host of emotions flitted across Bianca's face. Her features finally settled on irritation. Ash just wasn't sure where it was directed. He coughed gently and rolled his shoulder. "And he didn't come," she said in flat disappointment.

At the duke, then.

Ash exhaled. As long as he was admitting what he'd done, he'd be completely honest about what had happened next. She deserved the truth, and he planned to never keep secrets from her. "I wish I could say he at least responded, but he did not."

Bianca scowled, and her sister let out a surprising description of their brother, complete with a curse. Gasping in surprise, Bianca swung her gaze to the marchioness. They and the marquess promptly dissolved into laughter.

His mother joined them. "You look as though you're having a jolly time. Everyone is, I think. I should know, as I've spoken to everyone about St. Stephen's Day. Support for the event is overwhelming. Even from the viscount." She cast a look toward Thornaby, and Ash knew her well enough to recognize a thread of anger and distrust in her gaze.

The emotions stuck out to him because she rarely displayed them. However, Thornaby was a special case. When she'd learned Thornaby and the others were behind the house burning down, she'd been inconsolable. She revealed that she'd written to him and Keldon, sending a rider with the missives before speaking to Ash and Bianca. Then when they'd said no to requesting help, she hadn't wanted to admit she'd already done so. While Ash was ready to forgive, she hadn't yet reached that point. But Ash knew she would. She was far too kindhearted not to.

"Let us drink to the earl and his countess," Thornaby called out, raising his glass. "Buckleigh is a true hero—in every way. Without him, we would not be celebrating St. Stephen's Day this year as we ought."

Keldon lifted his glass. "Hear, hear!"

Ash felt the need to correct them. "Actually, if not for my lovely wife, there would be no St. Stephen's Day celebration this year. It is her passion and her drive that will continue this tradition." He gazed at Bianca with all the love overflowing his heart.

She smiled in return, her eyes promising a future filled with that same passion and drive. She lifted her glass in appreciation, and the room erupted in a chorus of "Hear, hear!" and "Congratulations!" and "To the earl and countess!"

Pride and joy filled Ash's chest as he drew Bianca against his side. As he looked around the room, he counted his blessings. "I wish the same happiness for all of you."

~

St. Nicholas Day was the official start to the Christmas season. Everyone celebrated in different ways, but the people of Hartwell had long made the day special by exchanging gifts among immediate family members. Bianca and Ash, along with her sister and her husband, spent the morning distributing gifts to the women and children who were not just in need of things but of good cheer. Bianca's heart swelled as she watched a young boy play excitedly with a half-dozen toy soldiers.

"This was a wonderful idea," Ash said softly as he came up beside her. "May I suggest we do it every year?"

She beamed up at him, glad that he shared her desire to help those in need. "Oh, I insist."

He chuckled. "Of course you do. I can imagine what you might say to my next suggestion."

"Please allow me to speak first," she said. "And I hope you don't think me too forward. I realize Shield's End was your house, but it was sitting empty, and Hartwell House is in horrible disrepair." A light sparked in his eyes, and she watched as his lips curled into a warm smile. "Is my proposal the same as yours?"

He lightly clasped her waist. "If you were going

to suggest we rebuild Shield's End as the new Institution for Impoverished Women, then yes. We are of the same mind. Again."

She laughed gaily. "I shouldn't have been surprised. We seem to want precisely the same things."

"Which is why we were destined to be."

She sighed, moving closer to him as he moved his hand around to her lower back. "Yes."

"I look forward to having the plans drawn up when we go to London next month."

"You're going to send inquiries before that?"

He nodded. "Next week. I know you're anxious to get started."

She glanced toward the people who would benefit from the new institution. "Now more than ever. And there should be a dedicated school with a teacher and a larger farm that will feed the occupants." She tipped her face up to meet his eyes. "Perhaps we could even build individual cottages for families."

"I couldn't agree more. Your heart is as beautiful as I remember." He brushed his lips across her brow. "Keldon has offered to oversee the building while I and Thornaby are in London for Parliament."

She riveted her gaze back to him, still in awe that he'd forgiven his tormentors so easily. Well, perhaps not easily. They'd discussed it at length, and she understood his reasons—they had everything to do with him and his sense of peace, not absolving the others' guilt. "You are the best of men."

"You make me want to be." He grimaced slightly. "I do wonder if you'll still think that when I tell you that I don't have a gift for you today. It's coming. I'm afraid that between the wedding and preparing for today, we've been quite busy."

Bianca laughed with relief. "Good, because I don't have your gift yet either." She lowered her voice. "But let me just say that I am confident we can think of plenty to give each other later. In our bedchamber."

He drew her into a shadowy corner and kissed her until they were both breathless. He stroked his finger along her cheek. "My love, you are the only gift I'll ever need."

Don't miss Poppy's story in The Gift of the Marquess! Then find out what happens with the St. Stephen's Day party and why Calder is such a Scrooge in Joy to the Duke! Coming in October and November 2019!

~

Thank you so much for reading The Red Hot Earl! It's the first book in my Regency holiday series, Love is All Around. I hope you enjoyed it!

Would you like to know when my next book is available and to hear about sales and deals? Sign up for my VIP newsletter at https://www.darcyburke.com/readergroup, follow me on social media:

Facebook: https://facebook.com/DarcyBurkeFans
Twitter at @darcyburke
Instagram at darcyburkeauthor
Pinterest at darcyburkewrite

And follow me on Bookbub to receive updates on pre-orders, new releases, and deals!

Need more Regency romance? Check out my other historical series:

The Spitfire Society - Meet the smart, independent women who've decided they don't need Society's rules, their families' expectations, or, most importantly, a husband. But just because they don't need a man doesn't mean they might not *want* one…

The Untouchables - Swoon over twelve of Society's most eligible and elusive bachelor peers and the bluestockings, wallflowers, and outcasts who bring them to their knees!

Wicked Dukes Club - six books written by me and my BFF, NYT Bestselling Author Erica Ridley. Meet the unforgettable men of London's most notorious tavern, The Wicked Duke. Seductively handsome, with charm and wit to spare, one night with these rakes and rogues will never be enough…

Secrets and Scandals - six epic stories set in London's glittering ballrooms and England's lush countryside, and the first one, Her Wicked Ways, is free!

Legendary Rogues - Four intrepid heroines and adventurous heroes embark on exciting quests across Regency England and Wales!

If you like contemporary romance, I hope you'll check out my Ribbon Ridge series available from Avon Impulse, and the continuation of Ribbon Ridge in So Hot.

I hope you'll consider leaving a review at your favorite online vendor or networking site!

I appreciate my readers so much. Thank you, thank you, *thank you*.

AUTHOR'S NOTE

One day last spring I thought it would be fun to write a Christmas trilogy and base the stories on classic holiday tales. What is more classic to a Gen X child like me than the stop motion TV special, Rudolph the Red-Nosed Reindeer? I had a lot of fun crafting a story that captured the moral of Rudolph and adding some romance. (Not that Rudolph and Clarice didn't have their thing!) You met Cornelius the butler who borrowed Yukon Cornelius's name and Harris the valet who I didn't name Hermie, but who wasn't right for his old job just like Hermie wasn't meant to be an elf. I loved incorporating them.

The Institution for Impoverished Women is something entirely of my own creation. It's based on workhouses of the time, but I didn't want a "real" workhouse which separated men and women (and children—they didn't see their parents often) and was typically more like a prison.

Thank you Catherine Kenner for the GOR-GEOUS rendition of The Red Hot Earl, sung to the tune of Rudolph the Red Nosed Reindeer (lyrics by me - spoiler: they are not as fabulous as her voice).

Listen to it here. Also thank you to Julie Kenner for, well, far too many things to list.

I hope you enjoyed this inspired story! And Merry Christmas. :)

Wicked Dukes Club

One Night for Seduction by Erica Ridley
One Night of Surrender by Darcy Burke
One Night of Passion by Erica Ridley
One Night of Scandal by Darcy Burke
One Night to Remember by Erica Ridley
One Night of Temptation by Darcy Burke

Secrets and Scandals

Her Wicked Ways
His Wicked Heart
To Seduce a Scoundrel
To Love a Thief (a novella)
Never Love a Scoundrel
Scoundrel Ever After

Legendary Rogues

Lady of Desire
Romancing the Earl
Lord of Fortune
Captivating the Scoundrel

Contemporary Romance

Ribbon Ridge

Where the Heart Is (a prequel novella)
Only in My Dreams
Yours to Hold
When Love Happens
The Idea of You

When We Kiss

You're Still the One

Ribbon Ridge: So Hot

So Good

So Right

So Wrong

The Untouchables Series

THE FORBIDDEN DUKE

"I LOVED this story!!" 5 Stars

-Historical Romance Lover

"This is a wonderful read and I can't wait to see what comes next in this amazing series..." 5 Stars

-Teatime and Books

THE DUKE of DARING

"You will not be able to put it down once you start. Such a good read."

-Books Need TLC

"An unconventional beauty set on life as a spinster meets the one man who might change her mind, only to find his painful past makes it impossible to love. A wonderfully emotional journey from attraction, to friendship, to a love that conquers all."

-Bronwen Evans, *USA Today* Bestselling Author

THE DUKE of DECEPTION

"...an enjoyable, well-paced story ... Ned and Aquilla are an engaging, well-matched couple –

strong, caring and compassionate; and ...it's easy to believe that they will continue to be happy together long after the book is ended."

-All About Romance

"This is my favorite so far in the series! They had chemistry from the moment they met...their passion leaps off the pages."

-Sassy Book Lover

THE DUKE of DESIRE

"Masterfully written with great characterization...with a flourish toward characters, secrets, and romance... Must read addition to "The Untouchables" series!"

-My Book Addiction and More

"If you are looking for a truly endearing story about two people who take the path least travelled to find the other, with a side of 'YAH THAT'S HOT!' then this book is absolutely for you!"

-The Reading Café

THE DUKE of DEFIANCE

"This story was so beautifully written, and it hooked me from page one. I couldn't put the book down and just had to read it in one sitting even though it meant reading into the wee hours of the morning."

-Buried Under Romance

"I loved the Duke of Defiance! This is the kind of book you hate when it is over and I had to make myself stop reading just so I wouldn't have to leave the fun of Knighton's (aka Bran) and Joanna's story!"

-Behind Closed Doors Book Review

THE DUKE of DANGER

"The sparks fly between them right from the start... the HEA is certainly very hard-won, and well-deserved."

-All About Romance

"Another book hangover by Darcy! Every time I pick a favorite in this series, she tops it. The ending was perfect and made me want more."

-Sassy Book Lover

THE DUKE of ICE

"Each book gets better and better, and this novel was no exception. I think this one may be my fave yet! 5 out 5 for this reader!"

-Front Porch Romance

"An incredibly emotional story...I dare anyone to stop reading once the second half gets under way because this is intense!"

-Buried Under Romance

THE DUKE of RUIN

"This is a fast paced novel that held me until the last page."

-Guilty Pleasures Book Reviews

" ...everything I could ask for in a historical romance... impossible to stop reading."

-The Bookish Sisters

THE DUKE of LIES

"THE DUKE OF LIES is a work of genius! The characters are wonderfully complex, engaging; there is much mystery, and so many, many lies from so many people; I couldn't wait to see it all uncovered."

-Buried Under Romance

"..the epitome of romantic [with]...a bit of danger/action. The main characters are mature, fierce, passionate, and full of surprises. If you are a hopeless romantic and you love reading stories that'll leave you feeling like you're walking on clouds then you need to read this book or maybe even this entire series."

-The Bookish Sisters

THE DUKE of SEDUCTION

"There were tears in my eyes for much of the last 10% of this book. So good!"

-Becky on Books...and Quilts

"An absolute joy to read... I always recommend Darcy!"

THE DUKE of KISSES

"Don't miss this magnificent read. It has some comedic fun, heartfelt relationships, heartbreaking moments, and horrifying danger."

"...my favorite story in the series. Fans of Regency romances will definitely enjoy this book."

THE DUKE of DISTRACTION

"Count on Burke to break a heart as only she can. This couple will get under the skin before they steal your heart."

"Darcy Burke never disappoints. Her storytelling is just so magical and filled with passion. You will fall in love with the characters and the world she creates!"

Secrets & Scandals Series

HER WICKED WAYS

TO LOVE A THIEF

"With refreshing circumstances surrounding both the hero and the heroine, a nice little mystery, and a touch of heat, this novella was a perfect way to pass the day."

–The Romanceaholic

"A refreshing read with a dash of danger and a little heat. For fans of honorable heroes and fun heroines who know what they want and take it."

-The Luv NV

NEVER LOVE A SCOUNDREL

"I loved the story of these two misfits thumbing their noses at society and finding love." Five stars.

–A Lust for Reading

"A nice mix of intrigue and passion...wonderfully complex characters, with flaws and quirks that will draw you in and steal your heart."

–BookTrib

SCOUNDREL EVER AFTER

"There is something so delicious about a bad boy, no matter what era he is from, and Ethan was definitely delicious."

-A Lust for Reading

"I loved the chemistry between the two main characters...Jagger/Ethan is not what he seems at all and neither is sweet society Miss Audrey. They are believably compatible."

-Confessions of a College Angel

Legendary Rogues Series

LADY of DESIRE

"A fast-paced mixture of adventure and romance, very much in the mould of *Romancing the Stone* or *Indiana Jones.*"

-All About Romance

"...gave me such a book hangover! ...addictive...one of the most entertaining stories I've read this year!"

-Adria's Romance Reviews

ROMANCING the EARL

"Once again Darcy Burke takes an interesting story and...turns it into magic. An exceptionally well-written book."

-Bodice Rippers, Femme Fatale, and Fantasy

"...A fast paced story that was exciting and interesting. This is a definite must add to your book lists!"

-Kilts and Swords

LORD of FORTUNE

"I don't think I know enough superlatives to describe this book! It is wonderfully, magically delicious. It sucked me in from the very first sentence and didn't turn me loose—not even at the end ..."

-Flippin Pages

"If you love a deep, passionate romance with a bit of mystery, then this is the book for you!"
  -Teatime and Books

CAPTIVATING the SCOUNDREL

"I am in absolute awe of this story. Gideon and Daphne stole all of my heart and then some. This book was such a delight to read."

-Beneath the Covers Blog

"Darcy knows how to end a series with a bang! Daphne and Gideon are a mix of enemies and allies turned lovers that will have you on the edge of your seat at every turn."

-Sassy Booklover

Contemporary Romance

Ribbon Ridge Series

A contemporary family saga featuring the Archer family of sextuplets who return to their small Oregon wine country town to confront tragedy and find love...

The "multilayered plot keeps readers invested in the story line, and the explicit sensuality adds to the excitement that will have readers craving the next Ribbon Ridge offering."

"Darcy Burke writes a uniquely touching and heart-warming series about the love, pain, and joys of family as well as the love that feeds your soul when you meet "the one.""

I can't tell you how much I love this series. Each book gets better and better.

"Darcy Burke's Ribbon Ridge series is one of my all-time favorites. Fall in love with the Archer family, I know I did."

Ribbon Ridge: So Hot

SO GOOD

" ...worth the read with its well-written words, beautiful descriptions, and likeable characters...they are flirty, sexy and a match made in wine heaven."

"I absolutely love the characters in this book and

the families. I honestly could not put it down and
finished it in a day."

SO RIGHT

"This is another great story by Darcy Burke.
Painting pictures with her words that make you
want to sit and stare at them for hours. I love the
banter between the characters and the general
sense of fun and friendliness."

" ...the romance is emotional; the characters are
spirited and passionate... "

SO WRONG

"As usual, Ms. Burke brings you fun characters and
witty banter in this sweet hometown series. I loved
the dance between Crystal and Jamie as they
fought their attraction."

"I really love both this series and the Ribbon Ridge
series from Darcy Burke. She has this way of
taking your heart and ripping it right out of your
chest one second and then the next you are
laughing at something the characters are doing."

ABOUT THE AUTHOR

Darcy Burke is the USA Today Bestselling Author of sexy, emotional historical and contemporary romance. Darcy wrote her first book at age 11, a happily ever after about a swan addicted to magic and the female swan who loved him, with exceedingly poor illustrations. Join her Reader Club at https://www.darcyburke.com/readerclub.

A native Oregonian, Darcy lives on the edge of wine country with her guitar-strumming husband, their two hilarious kids who seem to have inherited the writing gene. They're a crazy cat family with two Bengal cats, a small, fame-seeking cat named after a fruit, and an older rescue Maine Coon who is the master of chill and five a.m. serenading. In her "spare" time Darcy is a serial volunteer enrolled in a 12-step program where one learns to say "no," but she keeps having to start over. Her happy places are Disneyland and Labor Day weekend at the Gorge. Visit Darcy online at https://www.darcyburke.com and follow her social media: Facebook at http://www.facebook.com/darcyburkefans, Twitter @darcyburke at https://www.twitter.com/darcyburke, Instagram at https://www.instagram/darcyburkeauthor, and Pinterest at https://www.pinterest.com/darcyburkewrite.

Printed in Great
Britain
by Amazon